by the same author

MAKE ME A SOLDIER
AS FROM KEMMEL HILL
PORTRAIT OF A FAMILY FIRM

novels

THE HOUSE OF THE SPANIARD
UNLUCKY FOR SOME

THE *SAMARAI* AFFAIR

'How, in broad daylight, with no fog and no wind and no other ship within a mile, a First-Class pilot can put a comparatively small ship of seven thousand tons slap on the Revetment just passes my understanding.'

The ship, the *Samarai*, of the New Guinea Steamship Company, is insured for £750,000 but one of the marine insurance companies becomes suspicious and passes its file to the Liverpool CID. The few in the know are so tightly knit that the police find it hard to make the breakthrough.

ARTHUR BEHREND

The *Samarai* Affair

EYRE METHUEN

LONDON

First published 1973
Copyright © 1973 Arthur Behrend
Printed in Great Britain for
Eyre Methuen Ltd,
11 New Fetter Lane, EC4P 4EE by
Northumberland Press Ltd, Gateshead

SBN 413 45060 0

for Hester who thought of it
and for
Norman Morrison of the Pilotage
and Jack Rennie of the Police
with thanks for so much help

My thanks are also due
to Captain W. R. Colbeck R.N.R. and
Commander L. C. Hill O.B.E. D.S.C. R.D.
for allowing the use of the drawing
from the chart of Liverpool Bay

INTRODUCTION

This is a story of the time when the Mersey Docks and Harbour Board was in full swing and no one so much as dreamed that fifteen years later it would be swept away and replaced by the Mersey Docks and Harbour Company, a very different body however similar in name.

The meetings of the old Board took place weekly, as they had done for many years past. The place of meeting was and remains to this day the Dockboard building, also known as the Dock office – that copper-domed Edwardian pile standing four-turreted square on the southerly end of Liverpool's windswept Pier Head in too close proximity to the Italianate palace of Cunard and the architecturally ill-bred heights of the Royal Liver.

Sir Henry, his Company, his pilot, and his captain are fictitious, and there is no ship named *Samarai*. Of the other characters some are my friends – or were, for several are now dead – but I have of course given each a name different from his own. The two principal detectives are fictitious; so are all the policemen who come and go. The remaining characters, every woman included, are equally fictitious. On the other hand the background is as real as I have been able to make it, and every now and then, of the thousands of ships which pass in and out of the Port of Liverpool, one is unlucky enough to be caught and held by the Mersey Revetment.

Some fifteen years ago the following news item appeared in the *Liverpool Echo* of 8 September:

LIVERPOOL SHIP AGROUND ON REVETMENT

The 7,000-ton Liverpool motor vessel *Samarai* went aground in Crosby Channel shortly after 7 o'clock this morning. Tugs are now in attendance and a Dockboard spokesman states it is hoped to refloat her on the evening tide.

The *Samarai*, only 2 years old, is owned by the New Guinea Steamship Co. and was inward bound from Port Moresby and other New Guinea ports. The *Echo* understands the company's own pilot, Mr W. Gosling, was in charge of the vessel at the time of the grounding. Her Master, Captain I. Williams, resides in Rock Ferry. At the headquarters of the New Guinea Steamship Co. in India Buildings it was announced this morning that no member of the crew has been injured and the cause of the accident is at present unknown.

CHAPTER I

1

It was board-meeting day of the Mersey Docks and Harbour Board, and Sir Henry Hartley, a senior member and chairman of one of its more important committees, left his offices on the fourth floor of India Buildings in Water Street at seven minutes to one precisely. In spite of increasing portliness – he was now over sixty – he still preferred to walk down the marble stairway, and on reaching the ground floor he departed from the lofty and handsome central arcade by its exit into Brunswick Street. Here he thought it best to pause for a moment. He was not usually an unsociable man, but that day while walking to the Dockboard building he did not desire the company or conversation of two junior members likely to be converging on it at the same time from the same direction.

To his relief he saw neither, and he continued his sedate progress by the near pavement past the pub near the corner; there he stood waiting till the flow of traffic along Dock Road permitted him to cross. Another minute took him to the Dockboard building which he entered by its northern doorway. In the distance he saw several members stepping into the lift – on board-meeting days, much to the irritation of those of the Dockboard's large staff bound for their canteen on the top floor, two lifts were reserved for Members Only.

It was now three and a half minutes to one but Sir Henry saw no need to hurry. Beneath the dome in the central hall he walked, still with measured tread, directly across the coloured marble and mosaic patterned in the form of the points of the compass, and, like most others, he did not raise his head to read the message visible in letters of gold beneath the first-floor balcony which encircled the central hall THEY THAT GO DOWN TO THE SEA IN SHIPS THAT DO BUSINESS IN GREAT WATERS THESE SEE THE WORKS OF THE LORD AND HIS WONDERS IN THE DEEP.

Thus he reached the lifts. Having been saluted in naval fashion by two capped attendants dressed in the dark blue Dockboard uniform which made them appear more like chauffeurs than petty officers or commission-aires, he paused and stooped for a moment to address by name one of the Dockboard cats which was licking itself beside the lift – alone of the members he knew which Dockboard cat was which. On reaching the second floor the lift door was held open for him by the General Manager and Secretary's personal attendant, who emerged from his glass cage for that purpose on board days only. Sir Henry nodded to him as an old friend and walked along the synthetically-polished parquet corridor which led past the General Manager and Secretary's private office to the wing which contained the members' cloakrooms, luncheon room, and smokeroom, also the committee rooms and the boardroom itself.

The General Manager and Secretary's attendant viewed Sir Henry's departing back. 'He doesn't seem to be worrying much,' he remarked to the lift attendant.

On entering the private precincts, Sir Henry noted that Captain Coldstream, the Dockboard's Marine Surveyor and Water Bailiff, was waiting to have a word with him. A large man, Captain Coldstream looked exactly what he was – an ex-sailor of quality now holding down an exacting shore job to the complete satisfaction of everyone who had dealings with him.

'The *Salvor*'s there, Sir Henry, and I've six tugs standing by. We'll have a shot at getting her off at high water this evening.'

'Are they going to be successful?' Sir Henry was looking him straight in the eye.

'It's too early yet to say, sir. She was certainly well on when I saw her at nine o'clock this morning but it's a fairly high tide tonight and we may be lucky. I'm going back there after lunch.'

Sir Henry nodded and handed his soft black hat to the members' corridor attendant, who placed it unerringly on Sir Henry's personal peg. Sir Henry then opened the double swing doors of the boardroom and disappeared from public view. As usual he was the last to arrive.

The members' corridor attendant looked at the Marine Surveyor and said, 'I hope you get her off, sir. She's a fine ship from all I hear.'

The Marine Surveyor gave a noncommittal grunt, turned about, and hurried to his quarters on a higher floor.

Inside the ornate and generously-proportioned boardroom there was the usual muted hum of informal conversation which preceded every board meeting. Of the twenty-eight members twenty-one were present that day, and twenty were seated in comfortable armchairs round the sectional tables which together formed a horseshoe of gigantic size. The twenty-first, the chairman, was seated in the thronelike chair on the raised dais, insulated from others by the General Manager and Secretary on one side and by the Dockboard solicitor on the other. Representatives of the press, a mixed bag in ages but not in sex, were sitting in a row at the table between the dais and the members; they would depart silently through a side door once the public proceedings were over.

Members were still talking to their nearest neighbours when the one o'clock gun, then fired daily from the Birkenhead side of the Mersey, was heard. The chairman, an ageing man and a figurehead rather than a personality – a trader too and not a shipowner – looked round the big chamber at no one in particular and announced, 'Proceedings of the Docks and Quays Committee'. Hereupon the press held their pencils and pens poised in not very hopeful readiness for something worth reporting among the words which the Assistant Secretary, like an unfrocked clergyman at the lectern, began to read aloud and very fast. Thus the minutes of this particular committee – the essence, sometimes hardly recognizable, of its deliberations earlier in the week – were soon disposed of and another meeting of the board was well under way.

It ended twelve minutes later. Members, abandoning their order papers, rose as one and made off in twos and threes to the luncheon room upstairs. At last tongues were loosened, yet few spoke to Sir Henry. True the chairman hastened after him, took his arm up the stairs mainly for support, and said, 'I'm sorry, Harry. Everyone hopes it will end all right.' A couple of others mumbled the odd word of regret. Not that anyone was being unkind but at this stage there was really nothing to be said, and every member knew that Sir Henry, who was held in respect by most and in affection by one or two, was a man who did not wish for spoken sympathy.

Hence no one at the main table in the centre of the luncheon room mentioned the grounding, and, Sir Henry included, they talked of shooting, fishing, horseracing, and – by tradition – of everything except ships, politics, or trade.

But over in the corner furthest from the big windows there was a smaller overflow table where the members of the Pilotage Committee, an irreverent lot, liked to congregate, and it was here that the Pilotage Committee chairman, an outspoken shipowner named Rowley, was heard by one of the senior waitresses, handing vegetables at the time, to declaim to the table at large, 'How in broad daylight with no fog and no wind and no other ship within a mile a First Class pilot can put a comparatively small ship of seven thousand tons slap on the Revetment just passes my understanding.'

The waitress had gone when he said, 'Mind all you chaps turn up for the inquiry at next Tuesday's pilotage meeting.'

'I can't come,' said a well-filled shipbroker member named Arthur Bernard. 'I've got to be in London then.'

'Damn you,' said the Pilotage Committee chairman. 'Who else can't come?'

2

The Dockboard at that time still remained a stronghold of privilege and tradition, and in quite a few cases shipowner-members had succeeded their fathers and even grandfathers.* But the citadel was now yielding, and Sir Henry Hartley was not alone in having been elected to the Board on his merits and not on his birth. He concealed from no one that he had started work at the age of fifteen and his first job had been that of office boy in a Liverpool firm of shipping and forwarding agents.

He had left them in 1915 to join the King's Liverpool

* In the Dockboard smoking-room in the writer's time there existed several little lock-up compartments let neatly and almost invisibly into its panelled walls. Each contained its private stock of after-lunch cigars, the property of a few older members and of one or two younger ones. The lockers may be there to this day but I suspect they are now empty.

Regiment, won the Military Medal as a corporal, and been demobilized in 1919 with the rank of Captain. Instead of returning to his old firm he had then looked for something with better prospects, and found it in a shipowner's office close to the Cotton Exchange. Small and old-fashioned, the firm owned and managed two ships – reduced by war losses from four – which traded between Liverpool and New Guinea.

In after years it had become one of Sir Henry's aphorisms that success in life meant nothing more than being in the right place at the right time. The firm when he joined it consisted of two quiet and serious-minded brothers in partnership, and after a couple of years on the outward-freight desk he was asked one morning by the elder if he would like to go to New Guinea for a tour of duty. According to legend Harry replied, 'I'll go today, sir. After lunch.' A month later he went out to a tin shanty of an office in Port Moresby, and nine years later returned from a large brick-built one. The younger brother had just died and Henry was coming home to be made the junior partner. During those nine New Guinea years he had acquired or constructed wharves, warehouses, two copra factories, a timber mill with two thousand square miles of virgin forest, an oil refinery, and a half share in a reputable gold mine. Due to his achievements the firm, originally Shanklin Brothers, was now the New Guinea Steamship and Trading Company, and in addition to its trading interests owned seven deep-sea ships together with four shallow-draught tugs and a fleet of river craft in New Guinea.

In 1937 the elder Shanklin died, and Mr Henry, subject to the condition that he paid annuities to both the deceased partners' widows, became the senior partner. The younger brother's son, a mathematician of some distinction, remained his partner for a year, but withdrew from the firm and returned to Cambridge as a Fellow of his college. In 1940 Mr Hartley was summoned to the Ministry of Shipping, and there he stayed throughout the second war, mainly in sea transport. His services were outstanding and in 1946 he was rewarded with the KBE. By then he was back with his company, and within five years he had rebuilt its fleet and was thought by many to be on the direct line for a shipping peerage.

To his regret Sir Henry was childless – at any rate in Britain. His first wife, the daughter of a Liverpool police sergeant, was a splendid housewife, but she had died in childbirth. Nearly twenty years later he married again, this time the daughter of a colonel. She was seventeen years his junior, without warmth but a good horse-woman and of fragile beauty. To her occasional embarrassment he remained on the best of terms with his first father-in-law and with his married niece. His second father-in-law, who once had commanded a cavalry regiment, lived in North Wales as a minor squire and told his cronies that apart from brandy and cigars he and his son-in-law had nothing in common. It was believed that Sir Henry provided both fathers-in-law with financial support.

Sir Henry had long since realized his second marriage had been a failure. Almost from the start his sex-life with his wife was non-existent, initially because she feared having children, latterly because she neither cared enough for him nor desired it for herself. They were not sufficiently close to discuss the problem together. On the other hand neither wished to end the marriage – on her side the benefits of being a rich man's wife had overwhelming advantages. Hence, as can be the case with men and women of their particular period and of differing social backgrounds, they had settled down to live with each other in superficial amity combined with almost total mental and physical isolation. Yet Sir Henry was neither bitter nor dissatisfied. Ships and their business and the tangible rewards therefrom were the driving force of his life and his only real interest, and though in most respects a normal and apparently healthy man of sixty the absence of affection did not disturb him emotionally. He saw his wife for what she was – as in fact she did him – and notwithstanding the opportunities which arose from his frequent trips abroad he had discovered he could seldom be bothered to seek love elsewhere.

In business life though not a gambler Sir Henry was ready to take risks. He was courageous too, and the thing he feared most, due to abiding memories of his childhood and early youth, was poverty. Unlike many self-made men he was considerate to underlings but with others his temper could be short. Though he read the *Financial Times* he still preferred the *Mirror*. He was conscious of his position but by no means pompous; he was aware of his social failings and in that respect had not lost his sense of humour about himself. Yet he was not engaging, and most of those who fell foul of him considered him ruthless. On the other hand cats and children liked him.

He and his wife lived in Wirral in Ness Old Hall, and hitherto his means had been sufficient to maintain its ageing fabric and extensive gardens in good order. He was driven to Liverpool most days by his chauffeur; he disliked night driving and when compelled to attend one or other of Liverpool's too numerous business dinners he often preferred to engage a bedroom at the Adelphi. When in London he always stayed at the Ritz. He did not play bridge and refused to learn. Horses and hunting did not interest him; on occasions he shot or missed one of his father-in-law's pheasants and sometimes he was seen fishing the river which ran through the colonel's fields.

He was on the local board of a bank and of a London insurance company. Yet he was not a director of any of the great Liverpool companies which mattered, and few could say whether he had refused their invitations or not been asked. As a Dockboard member he was one of the nominees of the then all-powerful Liverpool Steamship Owners' Association, of which he had once been chairman for a year. He was too much of an autocrat to have proved a success.

Not long after the war New Guinea followed the example of India, Ghana, and a host of others by seeking independence. Sir Henry, a man more closely connected with its rival politicians than most, did not fail to read the writing on the wall, but like many others of importance in the world did not believe so backward a country could achieve its aspirations for many years. Due to conflicting powers at the United Nations and above all to the unexpected support of Indonesia the blow fell so suddenly that he was not prepared for the consequences.

Within a month of becoming a sovereign state New Guinea's first president, a clever, youngish half-caste named Albert Kikori, signed a decree which, contrary to strong British and Australian pressure and like Kaunda and the Zambian copper mines today, nationalized the fixed assets of the trading half of the New Guinea Steamship and Trading Company. The question of compensation was handled by the Commonwealth and Dominions Office but the infant republic possessed no resources other than a loan from China, the Australian army and air bases, a Dutch-owned brewery, a few British, Swiss, and Japanese bank buildings, a modern air-conditioned American hotel with two hundred and fifty bedrooms, and the vast properties of the New Guinea

Steamship and Trading Company. Hence the compensation offered, accepted, and finally paid was hardly enough to have furnished the first-class accommodation of an up-to-date passenger liner.

It must also be recorded that, ironic though it may seem, the rumour started in Port Moresby and spread from there in both directions throughout the populated areas of New Guinea's southern coast that Mr Kikori's father was Sir Henry Hartley. It is probable that Sir Henry knew of this rumour, but it gave him no concern. The past did not interest him, and his thoughts and entire life now revolved round the New Guinea Steamship Company and its salvation.

Having been a ready fighter since the age of six, Sir Henry's combative instincts had been aroused from the day his Company's troubles started. He knew its trading side had gone for ever and that its liner business, though still just viable, had no future. A change of direction was therefore essential, and he saw that the best hope of survival lay in switching from cargo ships to tankers. But he no longer had the cash with which to buy them. At that time the shipyards of Britain were hungry for orders, and for a start a mere half million would suffice. He was aware that while his personal reputation as a shrewd and competent ship-manager remained high, his Company was no longer considered credit-worthy by the City of London or by the lesser banking centres of the world. Too many eggs in one basket, the pundits had been saying, only financiers do not use simple words like that. His immediate problem had thus resolved itself into shortage of ready money. And not very much of that, because no more than half a million was needed. Could it not be found?

CHAPTER II

1

Sixteen miles out, in the Liverpool Bay area of the Irish Sea, the Bar Lightship is stationed to warn incoming ships that the entrance to Queens Channel, first leg of the twelve-mile long seaway which leads to the Port of Liverpool, lies three nautical miles ahead. Crosby Channel begins where Queen's Channel ends, and along its entire length the width of both channels is indicated on either side by buoys painted red for port, black for starboard, and spaced at frequent intervals. At night the buoys flash by automatic means. Within the channel there are several unmanned lightships which, like the Bar Lightship itself, swing with wind and tide. Occasionally the lightships, buoys too, are struck by some passing ship, and in exceptionally bad weather lightships and buoys alike are known to break away from their moorings. In places the seaway is narrow, and in Crosby Channel there is a sharp bend, almost a right-angle, which cannot be straightened because of surrounding sandbanks. Here, because of greater danger, the buoys are more closely spaced.

The rise and fall of the tide brings such quantities of sand from the sea and silt from the Upper Mersey that the channel requires constant dredging, and for that purpose a fleet of Dockyard dredgers works round the clock seven days a week. For miles the channels are contained on either side by vast training-banks of stone, brought and dumped there during the past hundred years by hopper barges from the quarries of North

Wales. These retaining walls, known as the Revetment, are in constant need of topping up and except at unusually low tides lurk underwater invisible to the eye.

Because of all these hazards and because no ship has yet been designed to steer as quickly or positively as a motorcar, an Act of Parliament has ordained that pilotage in the River Mersey is compulsory. Certain ships such as vessels of the Royal Navy are exempt, but few captains are bold enough to exercise this right. As for the rest, every ship's master irrespective of nationality knows that if he evades or even tries to evade the pilot boat on station, he is more than likely to be hauled up before the magistrates in Dale Street and heavily fined.

The Mersey, being also the only route to and from the Manchester Ship Canal, is a busy river, so busy that at the time of the events of this story it found full employment for 180 Mersey pilots, every one of whom had started his pilotage career by serving an apprenticeship of six or sometimes seven years aboard one of the four Mersey pilot boats. The pilot boats are largely manned by apprentice pilots, known as boathands, and Walter Gosling – now a senior and therefore First Class pilot – had become one in 1929 at the age of nearly eighteen.

The pilotage service is administered by the Pilotage Committee, which is well aware that all pilots are individualists since no other type of man would aspire to become one. It consists of eight nominated Dockboard members, two retired master mariners and four representatives of the pilots elected annually by the pilots themselves.

The majority of the Committee is also aware that, pleasant and co-operative though most pilots are as individual men, collectively they can be the very devil. This is partly because they belong to a guild which like most trade unions seeks for its members less work – that is to say a larger number of pilots – and more money. And since the cost of the service falls entirely on the ships which enter and leave the port, the Committee's duty in this as in other matters too is to hold the scales fairly yet firmly. This is not easy because the Committee is formed of two unequal and unequally vociferous halves often apt to talk and pull in different directions.

Since a committee can and on occasions must be remote, the key to a contented and disciplined service lies in the hands of its Superintendent, a man of many parts. A suitable paragon can usually be found; whether a Merseysider or not he will come from the splendid ranks of master mariners and is probably a man with deep-sea experience and the record of a number of successful years in command. Moreover he has to be astute enough in his knowledge of the sea and the world not to have wool drawn over his eyes by shipowners or pilots, and it goes without saying he must have the character and history of every pilot at his finger-tips.

2

How exacting is a pilot's job? What does he do each day? And how does he do it? ... The working life of Walter Gosling, the First Class pilot now in trouble over the *Samarai*, is one example.

In his earlier forties, in the best of health, and married for ten years, his wife had quickly discovered that owing to the exigencies of the service her husband could not make private engagements with any certainty of being able to keep them. At any hour of the day or night when on the outward rota he was liable to receive a telephone call ordering him to proceed to such and such a dock in Liverpool or Birkenhead or maybe to the terminus of the Ship Canal at Eastham Locks, and there, half an hour before high water, board the S.S. *Soandso*. When detailed for the inward rota his absences from home were likely to be longer, anything from a week to a couple of days. On such occasions he packed his bag and went off to the Pier Head to join the duty pilot boat, a trim ship moored alongside the landing stage and already flying the Boarding Flag, and until his turn came to board and pilot an inward-bound ship he would be living with twenty or more other pilots – some his friends and contemporaries, some neither – in the close confines and bodily proximities of the pilot boat. In effect a very small one-class passenger liner, she would be stationed off or cruising near Point Lynas, a headland on the exposed north-east tip of Anglesey, and thus subject to every wind that blew. When his time came to perform a pilotage he would get out of his bunk or put down his book or hand of cards or glass of beer and step overside into the boarding punt, a small-sized motor-boat manned by boathands as part of their training, to be transported to the ship he had to board.

Pleasant and easy work all this, so the landsman may think. And so it is on a calm summer day. But not so good in a gale or when the Mersey fogs come down. True that radar devices ashore and afloat make navigation in fog at least possible, but however clearly and brightly the course of the buoyed channel may be displayed on the radar screen and however big and unflickering the blob which signifies an approaching or following ship, it is never a certainty that each will pass or overtake the other safely. Every pilot knows that ships at close quarters tend to be drawn one to another, like toys floating in a child's bath.

The legal fact that the master is at all times responsible for the safety of his ship does not free the pilot from responsibility too. Nor in the event of an accident will it enable him to escape being summoned to appear before the Pilotage Committee to explain his actions and take the knock if held to blame. However urgently a ship may be required to dock, the pilot may consider it prudent to heave-to till the wind moderates or the fog clears, thereby missing a tide and perhaps delaying the start of the ship's discharge by a whole working day. On such occasions few masters would question or ignore a pilot's advice. At times, too, weather conditions are so bad that the boarding punt cannot leave the pilot boat to take off the pilot of an outward-bound ship; in consequence he may ultimately be landed at Cobh or Glasgow or a port in South Wales. He can even be carried to Las Palmas, as happened to Gosling within a month of his wedding.

So let anyone who envies the pilot his open-air and unconventional life imagine himself in Gosling's shoes and about to leave the warmth and comparative security of the pilot boat on a wild winter night to sit in the sternsheets of the punt now awaiting him in the so-called shelter of the pilot boat's lee. He is now aboard, and the punt crosses a quarter of a mile of heavy sea to the side of a ship which, having stopped her engines to pick him up, is rolling, pitching, or tossing – and sometimes doing all three at the same time. Standing up in the bucking punt and keeping his balance, his hand grasps the wet and half-frozen end of the rope-ladder let down for him from above – no ship lowers its accommodation ladder for a mere pilot – and chooses the moment when the punt is on the crest of the sea to swing himself across the foaming gap between the punt and the ship's side. His choice must be exact and his feet must be quick in finding and climbing the bottom rungs of the rope-ladder. Otherwise his legs will be crushed by the gunwale of the punt as it rises on the next wave.

All he now has to do is to climb the rope-ladder – his bag follows on a heaving-line – and ascend the run of iron ladders between the main deck and the bridge. He has accomplished what is technically known as a 'boarding', just one of the many thousand which every Mersey pilot has to perform throughout his service career.

On the bridge he will be greeted by the master or officer of the watch. If he finds in them an old acquaintance his welcome will be warm because he is the first link with port and brings the latest news from the water front, family and office news too. But should he find a stranger, a foreigner as likely as not, conversation will be confined to professional questions about tugs and draught and so on, answered in halting English mixed with any one of a dozen other languages. Thus a pilot's real work now begins, to end five to eight hours later when he has brought the ship to her destination. This may be into dock, alongside a jetty in the case of a tanker, or should the tide be out of step to a safe anchorage in mid-Mersey. Sometimes – more difficult for getting home, this – he takes her to Eastham Locks and hands her over to a Ship Canal pilot, a professional too but one whose working life is perhaps more sheltered.

The ship is now at rest, and Gosling picks up his bag and goes ashore, returning home to breakfast or to bed.

CHAPTER III

Unlike the Dockboard's other standing committees the Pilotage Committee meets in the pilotage office, situated close beside the edge of the Mersey on Canning pier head. Once upon a time schooners bringing granite kerbs for the streets of Liverpool unloaded in Canning Half-Tide Dock, and in Canning Dock itself there used to be a fish quay where trawlers discharged. But nowadays the only Trawler which remains is a pub on the dock road outside.

The pilotage office is a square building of Victorian-Gothic design constructed of weathered common brick picked out with glazed bricks round all its windows, and to shield its entrance hall from the prevailing winds its double doors face a different way from that which a visitor might expect. One or other wind seems to prevail continuously. Like bees or perhaps wasps entering and leaving their nest, the pilots themselves are the main door-users; their booking office is on the right downstairs. This is the domain of the Shoremaster, the man who allocates jobs to pilots.

Instead of a garden there is a narrow lawn of old cobbles ending a few yards from the double doors with a straight drop of six to thirty-five feet – according to the state of the tide – into the Mersey. The back door of the building opens into a yard used for the delivery of stores including food and drink for the Pilotage Committee's weekly lunches, and within fifty yards of the building there are two small graving docks, usually dry, and a wet dock filled to the brim with Mersey water. None is protected by anything more than a single low chain. Apart from these disadvantages, to which must be added the constant ringing of telephones in the Shoremaster's office, no quieter or more desirable residence exists on Merseyside.

Throughout the year the Pilotage Committee meets every Tuesday, except Christmas Day or Boxing Day if on a Tuesday, at 1.15 to the minute, and on all days the red and white pilot flag with the Board's crest in gold on a blue centre flies from the office flagstaff.

One sunny Tuesday during the autumn of this story the Committee's chairman, Mr Rowley, and Captain Armstrong, the Pilotage Superintendent, had been closeted together in the committee room since noon. As usual they had been discussing the agenda of the forthcoming meeting; furthermore the chairman's initials were required on various routine documents such as the week's expenditure of petty cash. In addition the case of the grounding of the *Samarai* was coming up that day in the form of the usual Inquiry, and in his quiet but authoritative voice Captain Armstrong had already said the pilot and all witnesses had been warned to attend and that so far as he knew all would attend. The big book containing the record of every Mersey pilot since the day he entered the service lay on the table, open at the page of W. G. Gosling, First Class pilot, who since February 1951 had been appropriated to the vessels of the New Guinea Steamship and Trading Company. As yet his history was for the chairman's eyes alone; it would not be made known to the committee members till the case was heard, judgement had been passed, and, if found to blame, the degree of punishment was being considered.

A minute or two before half-past twelve the chairman, tall and gaunt and still lame from a private plane accident that occurred many years before, got up stiffly from his chair and stalked into the luncheon room next door to join the committee members who were now quenching their pre-luncheon thirsts. Four of the eight nominated Dockboard members were present, among them Mr Bernard the shipbroker. He had got out of his London visit. Another nominated member, a shipowner named Mr James, would not appear till lunch was half over, a habit which his friends attributed to over-zeal for work and not to unpunctuality. The two retired master mariners, a pair of likeable and friendly men and both of course captains, were also present; they acted as the committee's technical assessors and were assiduous in their attendances. All looked inquiringly at the chairman as he entered – by now the *Samarai* had become big news. But he was saying nothing and like any man who needs a drink and feels he has earned one he made for the row of bottles on the side table and mixed a pink gin. While drinking he glanced at the clock, a cue taken by the uniformed steward who pressed the button of an unseen but not unheard buzzer, and from the floor above an old-fashioned food lift loaded with cover dishes came noisily down and filled the luncheon room with appetizing smells. The seven lunchers sat down.

Mr Rowley sat at the head of the table. It was known that he still suffered pain from his accident. In speech he was often impish and devastating, and for that reason some feared him. His patience in committee was not inexhaustible nor could he invariably put witnesses at their ease. But in grip and fairness he was beyond criticism, and of all the Dockboard's 28 members not one would have made a better chairman for this coming inquiry. Moreover no member of the Pilotage Committee, the pilots' representatives included, anticipated that he, like some chairmen they had tolerated, would waste anyone's time or allow proceedings to get out of hand.

At 1.15 on the dot cigarettes were stumped out, coffee cups drained, and the lunchers, now joined by Mr James, filed into the committee room. There they found all four of the pilots' representatives awaiting them; they were studying the large-scale model which occupied the centre of the big oval table. It was made of painted wood and represented the approaches to the Port of Liverpool. Up against the acute bend of Crosby Channel an out-of-scale model hull, also made of wood, marked the present resting-place of the *Samarai*.

By the exchange of nods and brief greetings the committee temporarily unified itself and seated itself round the table with its chairman in the middle, the rest on either side of him in order of seniority. The pilots' representatives sat in order of seniority too, and like the opposition in the House of Commons they signified their solidarity by sitting together.

The finer the day outside the darker the committee room, a paradox due to its windows overlooking the Mersey. Scenically the view was superb but the light reflected from the river was often so strong that members whose chairs faced the windows were apt to complain they could see neither the witnesses nor the model; hence on bright afternoons the Superintendent anticipated grumbles by pulling down the blinds. The committee room's walls were sprinkled with framed photographs, some more faded than others, of past pilot boats and past chairmen; in their midst, and as out of place as a saxophone among violins, hung a modernistic portrait in oils of the latest pilot boat, an unsolicited gift from its builders. No one liked it.

Financial statements, such as pilotage earnings for the week just past, were lying on the table, and one or two members glanced at them while the first item of business was being disposed of – the consideration of tenders for the provision of new Manila ropes for the pilot boats and further tenders for the consequent sale of what the new displaced. These latter were particularly low, and anyone versed in committee work knows how much dissent and heat can be engendered by trivialities such as money for old rope.

As the second item on the agenda a veteran pilot on the point of retirement was ushered into the room to receive from the chairman the committee's thanks for forty years of blameless service. Clearly more at home on a ship's bridge than confronting the Pilotage Committee, he answered the chairman's benevolent question by saying he couldn't recall having been summoned to appear before it before. But that, he added quickly, was more due to luck than to merit, and amid the murmured good wishes of all he withdrew.

Next, two youngsters made their formal appearance to be confirmed in their appointment as junior boat-hands, one a bright lad with fuzzy red hair, the other dark and serious. The chairman asked if any member had a question to put to them; Mr Clay, a shipowner who thought in terms of great rather than narrow waters, came out with his favourite, 'Why on earth do you *want* to be a pilot?' Not a bad question; the answers, often surprising, ranged from, 'Because my father is one, sir,' to 'Because when I get married I wouldn't want to be too far away from home.'

Having thus ticked over gently during the previous ten minutes, the committee had now run itself in for the major business of the afternoon, and at a nod from the chairman the committee clerk went outside to shepherd in the pilot and four witnesses.

When the sorting out and shuffling of feet had ended

the chairman invited the witnesses to sit down in the chairs provided. The pilot, briefed beforehand by the Superintendent, stepped forward smartly towards the table and took up his stand facing the chairman; by the unwritten rules of these occasions he was dressed in a dark blue suit with a black tie.

A dozen pairs of eyes glanced and in some cases stared at him: they saw a man who looked resilient and tough, and who even in his present surroundings showed no sign of nervousness. Like many other pilots of middle-age his cheeks were sallow, confirming that the hardships of a life of such irregular hours more than cancelled out the benefit of sea-breezes.

Two of the witnesses wore merchant navy uniform; of these one was a Chief Officer, the other a Third. The other two witnesses were in civilian clothes; the short stocky man with thin black hair could only be the ship's captain, the burly and rubicund one its quartermaster.

All four were now seated in varying degrees of discomfort, and the chairman addressed them, saying pleasantly and informally, 'Thank you for coming to help us. I want to tell you, in case you don't already know, that this is a Pilotage Committee inquiry and nothing else, and we are here to learn the facts of what happened so that we can judge whether or not our pilot was to blame, and if so to what extent. This is not a court of law. No one is on oath, and whatever you tell us will remain within these four walls. In other words anything you say will not be used or repeated should there be any later inquiry such as in your company's office or in the Admiralty Court. You will be entitled to ask the pilot questions after he has given evidence, and in the same way he is entitled to question you. I hope I have made myself clear and that you gentlemen will now help us to arrive at the truth.'

'Indeed we will, sir!' It was the captain who had spoken, and the words which shot out of his mouth like bullets from a gun so startled Mr Bernard, the readiest member to take a nap, that he opened his eyes and did not close them again.

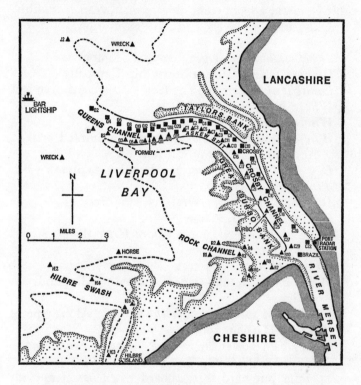

LIVERPOOL BAY

The Samarai *grounded in Crosby Channel E.N.E. of C.6 buoy (see pilot's report on pages 34 & 35). This buoy is shown immediately below the S of TAYLORS BANK.*

'Let us have Mr Gosling's report,' the chairman had just said to the committee clerk.

The printed form in the committee clerk's hand had been completed with entries in the pilot's writing. Though not an easy document to read aloud the committee clerk, a competent elderly man, read it audibly, quickly, and – properly – without expression:

Vessel's name and rig, 'Samarai', motor vessel
Owners, New Guinea Steamship Company
Draught of Water Aft, 27 feet   *Forward,* 26 feet
Where boarded, Point Lynas
Where bound, Gladstone Dock
Where Casualty occurred, Vessel grounded on
    Revetment E.N.E. of C.6 Red Buoy
Day and Date of Casualty, Tuesday, September 8th
Time, 07.48 B.S.T.
Direction of Wind, Westerly   *Force,* 1
State of Weather, Fine
Time of Tide, 3 *hours before High Water, H. W.*
    being 10.36
Height of Tide, 27 feet
What look-out, and where placed? All hands on
    stations
Course and speed through the water, Along line of
    buoys. Harbour speed
Under own power, or in tow? Under own power
Measures taken, and when, to avoid collision,
    Helm put hard to starboard when vessel ran out
    of Channel. Anchors let go.
Cause of Casualty,
    I boarded the vessel off Point Lynas and proceeded
    in normal way to Bar Lightship. On passing Bar
    Lightship at 07.04 engines put to Stand By, crew
    ordered to harbour stations, anchors made free for

34

running. I proceeded up-Channel in clear visibility. At C.3 Buoy I gave order Starboard a Little, and steadied up with C.5 Buoy on my starboard bow. When abreast of C.5 I ordered Starboard Easy, to pass C.7 and C.9 on my starboard side. The vessel did not respond to my second order and continued across Channel and grounded behind C.6.

The committee clerk sat down.

THE CHAIRMAN (to Mr Gosling): You see the big model in front of you, also the small one which represents your ship. Please take the small model and show us your course, starting at the entrance to Queens Channel ... Use the model please, not your finger, and remember we all want to see.

MR. GOSLING (doing as told): It was here at C.3 I ordered 'Starboard a Little', but soon after that and as she wasn't steadying up properly I told the quartermaster —

CHAIRMAN: Has the ship manual or telemotor steering?

MR GOSLING: Telemotor, sir.

CHAIRMAN: Go on.

MR GOSLING: I told the quartermaster to give her a bit of port. She then steadied up to some extent but I didn't altogether like her position when she got abreast of C.5. That was when I ordered 'Starboard Easy' —

QUARTERMASTER (tersely, while bending forward to see): If you'd let me alone I'd have —

CHAIRMAN: Don't interrupt. I've told you you can ask questions when he's finished evidence. (to Mr Gosling) Go on.

MR GOSLING: She didn't seem to respond to 'starboard easy' —

CHAIRMAN: What do you mean by 'seem to'? Either she

did respond or she didn't. Which do you mean?

MR GOSLING: She didn't respond, sir.

CHAIRMAN: And then?

MR GOSLING: She ran out of the Channel and grounded.

CHAIRMAN: Have you any complaint about the way the telemotor gear was working?

MR GOSLING (after a slight pause): No sir, I can't say I have. She'd been answering her helm normally up to then.

CHAIRMAN: Then how on earth do you account for her running out of the Channel?

MR GOSLING: The trouble began between C.3 and C.5 when she wasn't steadying up.

CHAIRMAN (to each committee member in turn): Any question?

FIRST FIVE MEMBERS: No, sir.

CAPTAIN BLACK (the senior assessor): When exactly did you order the anchors to be let go and reverse the engines?

MR GOSLING: The moment her bow ran out of the Channel.

CAPTAIN BLACK: Why did you not give this order sooner?

MR GOSLING: Because till then I felt confident the ship was going to answer the starboard helm. And I knew if I let them go too soon she couldn't have helped running out of the Channel.

CAPTAIN BLACK (to chairman): That's all, sir.

CHAIRMAN (to remaining members): Any more questions?

MR HARRISON (senior representative of the pilots): Yes, sir. (to Mr Gosling) How long have you been appropriated to the New Guinea Steamship Co.?

MR GOSLING: Five and a half years.

MR HARRISON: Is this the first time you have been involved in any kind of accident with their ships?

MR GOSLING: Yes.

MR HARRISON: Nothing further, sir.

CHAIRMAN (to quartermaster): If you have a question to ask the pilot you may ask him now.

QUARTERMASTER: I want to know if he's blaming me for this.

CHAIRMAN: Ask him, not me.

QUARTERMASTER (to Mr Gosling): Are you?

MR GOSLING: Certainly not.

QUARTERMASTER: Then who are you blaming?

CHAIRMAN (to Mr Gosling): There's no need to answer that. (to quartermaster) Have you any other question?

QUARTERMASTER (still tense): Not to ask the pilot, sir. But I've something to say myself.

CHAIRMAN: You will have the opportunity to give evidence later. (to committee clerk) Who's the next witness?

COMMITTEE CLERK: The Third Officer, Mr Livesey. He was on the bridge when the vessel went aground.

CHAIRMAN: Will you stand up and come forward to the table? Is there anything additional you can tell us?

MR LIVESEY: If you want my opinion, sir, I think the pilot was late in ordering 'starboard easy'.

CHAIRMAN: Your opinion is of value but you have to remember he and not you was in charge of the ship.

MR LIVESEY: That's true, sir. But it's still my opinion.

CHAIRMAN (to Mr Gosling): Have you any question to ask the Third Officer?

MR GOSLING: No, sir.

CHAIRMAN: I see the Chief Officer is a witness. (to Chief Officer) Where were you at the time of the grounding?

CHIEF OFFICER (standing up): On the fo'c'sle head, sir. That is my harbour station.

CHAIRMAN: Then presumably all you can tell us is about the anchors?

CHIEF OFFICER: That's right, sir. They'd been made free for running when we passed the Bar Lightship. There was no delay in letting them go, and they ran freely.

CHAIRMAN: Is there anything else you wish to tell us?

CHIEF OFFICER: Only that I agree with the Third Officer when he said he thought the pilot was on the late side in ordering 'starboard easy'. I had the same impression because she wasn't following the line of buoys as closely and quickly as I expected. But I didn't feel uneasy.

CHAIRMAN: Thank you. (to Mr Gosling) Any questions?

MR GOSLING: None, sir.

CHAIRMAN (to Captain Williams, ship's master): I understand you did not reach the bridge till the ship had actually grounded?

CAPTAIN WILLIAMS: That is right, sir.

CHAIRMAN: Then we'll hear the quartermaster next. (to quartermaster) Come forward to the table, please.

QUARTERMASTER (rising quickly): Thank you.

CHAIRMAN: Were you at the wheel at the time?

QUARTERMASTER: I was, sir.

CHAIRMAN: Then what have you to tell us?

QUARTERMASTER: She's always been a handy ship, like she was then too. If he'd left me alone I could have kept her steady round the buoys like I've done many a time before. 'Come along, Quartermaster, steady her up and get a bit more port on her,' he says to me as we come round C.3, and what's more he says it twice. He never ought to, he just confused me.

CHAIRMAN: But the pilot has told us she needed steadying after passing C.3.

QUARTERMASTER: She was a deep ship and may have done, but nothing like what he says. To listen to him you'd think she was jigging about all over the place. She wasn't jigging at all. Forgive me for speaking blunt, sir, but it was a damned shame, that's what it was —

CHAIRMAN (raising hand to silence him): You did as you were told, Quartermaster, and no one will blame you for that.

QUARTERMASTER: Some will, sir.

CHAIRMAN (to Mr Gosling): Have you a question to ask this witness?

MR GOSLING: One, sir. (turning to quartermaster) You agree she wanted steadying when she came round C.3? And that, being fully loaded, she needed a heavy swing?

QUARTERMASTER: All ships whether fully loaded or not need steadying coming round a bend like that. But you've always left it to me before, same as you could have done last Tuesday.

MR GOSLING (to chairman): Nothing more, sir.

No member, the assessors and pilots' representatives included, wished to question the quartermaster, and the chairman told him he could sit down. He did, reluctantly.

CHAIRMAN: Now, Captain Williams, what have you to tell us? Come forward, please.

CAPTAIN WILLIAMS (speaking with a strong Welsh accent): I had left the bridge about fifteen minutes previously and gone to my cabin to complete my portage bills. The door was open and I heard Mr Gosling order the quartermaster to give her a bit of port but thought nothing of it. Indeed sir, I had no reason to feel apprehension because Mr Gosling knows this ship and has brought her in many times before and with the same quartermaster at the wheel. The quartermaster's a good man, sir. I could not

39

believe my ears when I heard the orders 'Hard a star-board' and 'Let go the anchors' in almost the same breath, and I darted from my cabin and the impact of her hitting the Revetment knocked me off my feet and I fell flat. By the time I was on my feet again it was all over.

CHAIRMAN: As you weren't on the bridge there's really no light you can throw on this?

CAPTAIN WILLIAMS: I can tell you this, sir. I just can't make head or tail of it. It's as though he put her on the Revetment on purpose.

CHAIRMAN (very sternly): You have no right to say a thing like that.

CAPTAIN WILLIAMS: I have to get it off my chest, sir. He's put paid to my ship.

CHAIRMAN: Captain Williams, everyone here sympathizes with you over that. (to Mr Gosling) Do you wish to ask any questions?

MR GOSLING: No, sir.

CHAIRMAN: Does any member wish to question Captain Williams?

MR HARRISON (pilots' senior representative): I have just two, sir. (to Captain Williams) You have told us you were in your cabin, and please don't think I'm criticizing you for having gone there. But may I take it you would not have been there unless you had had the fullest confidence in Mr Gosling and in your Third Officer?

CAPTAIN WILLIAMS: My Third Officer has nothing to do with this. He wasn't in charge unfortunately –

MR HARRISON: Please answer my question. May I take it you would not have gone to your cabin had you not had full confidence in Mr Gosling?

CAPTAIN WILLIAMS: Of course I would not.

MR HARRISON: Has Mr Gosling handled your ship to

your satisfaction on all previous occasions during the time he has been your Company's appropriated pilot?

CAPTAIN WILLIAMS: Sir Henry would have heard quick enough if he had not.

MR HARRISON: Thank you, Captain Williams. That is all I wanted to know. (to chairman) No more questions, sir.

The inquiry now ended. The witnesses were again thanked by the chairman for attending, asked to withdraw, and told they could go away. The pilot was told to withdraw and wait outside the room.

CHAIRMAN (as soon as pilot and witnesses had left the room): Quiet please, everyone. This may be a remarkable case but it does not seem to me a difficult one. Captain Black, what do you think of the pilot's behaviour?

CAPTAIN BLACK: Well, sir, the pilot obviously made a serious error of judgement, in all the circumstances a surprising one for a man of his experience to make. I think he did fluster the quartermaster, but he said the ship hadn't steadied and the quartermaster corroborated him over that, at any rate up to a point. Why, according to the pilot, she needed so much steadying I can't say, except that ships can and do behave unexpectedly at times, and with the flood tide behind him this may have been one of them. One other thing. The pilot was right in the explanation he gave as to why he didn't let his anchors go sooner, but why he appears to have waited so long before ordering 'Hard a starboard' I can't say. The ship may have been well out of control by then, and in that event I don't think he could have saved her by giving the order earlier. There's very little room to manoeuvre in that narrow part of the Channel.

CHAIRMAN (to Captain Green, the other assessor): And what do you think?

CAPTAIN GREEN: Bearing in mind he had a deep ship I think the pilot gave his second 'Starboard easy' order too late. That was when the trouble really started, and to that extent he is guilty of an error of judgement, a very serious one as the consequences have shown. For the rest I agree with Captain Black.

The chairman now went round the table, asking each member in turn if he agreed or disagreed with the opinion of the assessors, and if he had anything he wished to add. Two members agreed and said they had nothing to add, and then:

A MEMBER (a trader, not a shipowner): Of course he's to blame. I think he must have been drunk.

MR HARRISON (with heat): We take very great exception to that. His sobriety was not questioned by a single witness. Why start that kind of red herring now?

THE MEMBER: Because I can't think of any likelier explanation to account for what he did. I have a hundred tons of copra in that ship –

CHAIRMAN (scathingly): That is at least one valid reason why your opinion is of no value to us.

Two more members agreed with the assessors and did not wish to add anything, and then:

MR BERNARD: I agree with Captain Black and Captain Green. But since no one else has mentioned it I should like to say I was impressed by the quartermaster and by the way he gave evidence. Why did the pilot apparently go out of his way to fuss him? There may be a bit more in this than meets the eye –

CHAIRMAN (tapping his gavel on the table and looking towards the pilots' representatives): Do you four agree that this accident was caused by the pilot's error of judgement?

MR HARRISON: I think the quartermaster by not steadying up the ship was also to blame.

CHAIRMAN: We are not here to pass judgement on the quartermaster. Do you find the pilot to blame or not to blame?

MR HARRISON: If you put it like that –

CHAIRMAN: I do put it like that.

MR HARRISON: Then I consider the pilot partly but not wholly to blame.

Two of the pilots' representatives agreed with him that the pilot was partly but not wholly to blame; the fourth representative held that the pilot was not to blame.

CHAIRMAN (to fourth representative): Implying that the ship just took it into her head to run herself aground?

FOURTH REPRESENTATIVE: I didn't say that, sir.

CHAIRMAN: My own opinion is that the pilot was wholly to blame. That means eleven members of the Committee find him wholly or partly to blame, one finds him not to blame. Please tell us his record.

SUPERINTENDENT: It is entirely clean except for one entry fifteen years ago when he was a Second Class pilot. (reading from record of service book) He then appeared before the Committee for not having boarded an outgoing ship in Liverpool at the time ordered. The Committee, having considered his explanation that his motorcar refused to start and that he lost time by having to telephone for a taxi, cautioned him.

CHAIRMAN: Thank you.

SUPERINTENDENT: There is a further entry. In April 1948 he appeared before the Committee to receive its congratulations on having been awarded a certificate of the Royal Humane Society. During the previous winter he had rescued a senior boathand who fell overboard in a rough sea from the bows of the boarding craft transporting Mr Gosling from No 2 Pilot Boat in the vicinity of Point Lynas to the Swedish steamer *Dahlia*.

CHAIRMAN: Thank you.

SUPERINTENDENT: In fairness to Mr Gosling and seeing that someone has questioned his sobriety, may I say I understand he is a teetotaller? Up to now he has been considered a very good pilot.

CHAIRMAN: Thank you. (to committee members) We must now decide what to do with him.

A pilot found to blame may be dealt with in a number of ways ranging from dismissal from the service to a reprimand, sometimes to a mere caution. Pilots are rarely dismissed, and only in the case of extreme misconduct such as drunkenness when on duty. For a professional mistake – usually termed an error of judgement – a pilot, if his error is grave, may be suspended for a time or reduced in rank or severely reprimanded. For minor errors of judgement a reprimand is the usual penalty, or, if the Committee is on the verge of giving him the benefit of the doubt, a caution. A pilot's previous record is always taken into account, and in arriving at a decision, particularly in cases where differences of opinion are likely to be wide, the chairman, not wishing to give a lead himself, may first ask each member of the committee to give his opinion in turn. That is what he preferred to do on this occasion, and he started with the junior member and worked upwards.

CHAIRMAN (to Mr Gough, a coastal shipowner who though the newest member happened to be the oldest): What do you say?

MR GOUGH: As you know, sir, I haven't much experience here but I should say it's a case for suspension at the very least. From the evidence I don't think he has a leg to stand on.

CHAIRMAN: Thank you. (to the member who had suggested the pilot was drunk) What do you say?

THE MEMBER: Sack him. We can't have a man like that loose on the river.

CHAIRMAN: Mr James?

MR JAMES (a wise and thoughtful shipowner): I don't agree about sacking him. You can't do that for an error of judgement, however serious. Nor do I care for suspension because I don't like taking away a man's income, even for a month or two. But I think this is a case where the penalty must be severe, and I suggest reducing him in rank.

CHAIRMAN: How far?

MR JAMES: I'm afraid I haven't given that any thought yet. Perhaps to Second Class pilot.

CHAIRMAN (to Mr Bernard): Will you now say?

MR BERNARD: I like Mr James' suggestion best. From the evidence the pilot lost his grip completely and I'm still puzzled why.

CHAIRMAN (to Mr Clay): What about you?

MR CLAY: I think this is a bad case and I agree with Mr James.

The chairman next asked the assessors. Captain Black said it was a serious offence and in his opinion the pilot should be severely reprimanded and also reduced in rank. Captain Green said, 'I agree'. It was now the turn of the pilots' representatives, and the chairman asked Mr Harrison, the senior.

MR HARRISON: I'd agree to a severe reprimand, but not more.

CHAIRMAN (to pilots' second representative): You?

SECOND REPRESENTATIVE: I agree with Mr Harrison, sir.

CHAIRMAN (to pilots' third representative): And you?

THIRD REPRESENTATIVE: Same with me, sir.

CHAIRMAN (to pilots' fourth representative): What about you?

FOURTH REPRESENTATIVE: I don't agree, sir. I've already said I don't find the pilot to blame. You can't punish him for someone else's mistake.

CHAIRMAN: Thank you. (to committee as a whole) My own view is that this is the most serious error of judgement which has occurred here for a long time, and in saying this I disregard the consequences of his mistake and the fact that the ship is still on the Revetment and likely to break her back. As one member said, 'We can't have a pilot like that loose on the river', but I qualify that by adding, 'in charge of larger ships'. In my opinion and in spite of his previous good record he should be severely reprimanded and reduced in rank not to Second Class pilot as Mr James suggested, but to Third Class pilot.

MR HARRISON: I think that's too much, sir.

SEVERAL MEMBERS OF COMMITTEE (almost in unison): I don't.

CHAIRMAN: I now ask you to vote on my proposal. I'm prepared to tell the pilot this is not necessarily a permanent reduction and that he can reinstate himself in time to come by not making further mistakes. (to pilots' representatives) Whether you like it or not, we have to face it he put a fair-sized modern ship on the Revetment under perfect conditions and without any mitigating circumstances beyond the half-hearted suggestion that the quartermaster didn't steady her up.

46

The voting, by show of hands, followed at once. Eight voted in favour of a severe reprimand and reduction to Third Class pilot, four against.

CHAIRMAN: Carried by a majority. (to committee clerk) Ask Mr Gosling to come in.

The committee clerk opened the door and Mr Gosling is brought in.

CHAIRMAN: Mr Gosling, by a majority the Committee has decided you are to be severely reprimanded and reduced to Third Class pilot. You know better than we do what went on in your mind and what you did or didn't do to cause this accident. You gave your evidence frankly, I give you credit for that. We are also aware that hitherto your record as a pilot has been excellent. For that reason you will not necessarily remain a Third Class pilot for the rest of your service. That is entirely up to you.
MR GOSLING: I understand, sir.
CHAIRMAN: Thank you, Mr Gosling. That is all.

Mr Gosling withdrew, and the meeting broke up. On the way out one or two members paused in the luncheon room for another drink; the majority did not. As the members went down the stairs several of the pilots' representatives were seen commiserating with Mr Gosling, and by the double exit doors Mr Bernard was overheard to remark to Mr James, 'Well, compared with most inquiries it's been quite a party.'

CHAPTER IV

1

After the inquiry Walter Gosling drove straight home. The ordeal had so drained his emotions that for the first mile he had no thoughts at all.

Then as his natural resilience began reasserting itself a series of flashbacks came tumbling through his mind and he saw himself vividly at the start of his career. As a boathand he'd had no difficulty in passing the yearly examinations in seamanship and on the geography and whims of the Mersey and his record in the pilot boats had been exemplary. He'd won several swimming races in the annual competitions between the pilot boats, and when on leave ashore his only interest lay in sport, no one minding if his favourite one was racing – horses first and greyhounds second. Nor had he found it a handicap that his uncle, a retired and respected First Class pilot, still had friends in the service.

His air of purpose impressed the Pilotage Committee, so he'd been told, when on appointment as Third Class pilot he made his formal appearance before it. Two uneventful years followed and he was promoted to Second Class pilot, thereby being permitted to handle bigger and deeper ships and thus earn more money. Next, thanks to the war and a string of retirements, he'd become a First Class pilot in his early thirties and handled still bigger ships and earned round about two thousand. His navigational record remained clean and he hadn't been involved in any collision or incident. His hobby was still betting, and by now he was known throughout the service as a compulsive and on the whole successful punter. As a steady and reliable pilot too.

It was then he met Kath. They first spoke to one another at his cousin's wedding, and it must have been a case of unlike being attracted to like because he was no extrovert and she was. Moreover he was slight whereas she was tall and big and interested in operatics and possessed a good soprano voice. He'd told her he was a betting man and promised to stop; she told him of her stage ambitions and undertook to put them aside. They married when the war was over – he'd been lucky there because not every Mersey pilot had survived its perils – and the Superintendent of Pilotage and nine pilots came to their wedding. And Harry Hartley – he'd not become Sir Henry then – came too.

For Gosling as for a score of other First Class pilots further promotion lay ahead. One by one and as opportunity arose each was invited to become the appropriated pilot of one of the larger companies whose volume of trade and frequence of service justified the removal of its pilot from the ordinary rota, thus freeing him to meet his owner's incoming ships whenever they arrived off the Mersey and when outward bound conduct them from dock to the limits of pilotage.

Appropriation brings with it more than prestige and has long been sought after because by custom an owner pays his appropriated pilot a private annual retainer, the amount varying according to the means and generosity of the individual owner. Yet, human nature being what it is, the rank and file of the service dislike the system; they hold that all First Class pilots should be equal and challenge the shipowner's time-honoured right to maintain that some are safer and more skilled than others. He'd thought that way too – till he became one ... An extra two-fifty a year, that's what it had been worth to

49

him. But as things had panned out it would have been a damned sight better if he'd never been asked –

He braked abruptly. He was all but home now, back in the present too, and he swung his fine new Ford through his open gateway and over the concrete into the garage. Thank heaven there's no mortgage or HP on any of this little lot, he thought as he closed the garage doors and went round by the back. He entered the kitchen; there was Kath, stirring something on the gas-ring.

'Well?' she asked, still stirring.

He stared at her, aware how desirable she was and how fiercely he wanted to seize her in his arms and kiss her ... No, no, not now, he told himself in dumb misery and a surge of rising fear and shame. For years they'd been in the habit of talking over important things in bed before making love and while each felt happy and relaxed, yet so far he hadn't faced up to telling her the biggest of them all ... Oh God, she'd have to be told soon, before she guessed ... And what then?

'Well?' she asked again, her voice sharp with anxiety.

'That's it,' he answered. 'We've had it.'

'Dismissed from the service?'

He half laughed. 'For a "grave error of judgement"? No, of course not. Reduced to Third Class and severely reprimanded.'

'So what?'

'Well, we needn't be here much longer.'

'I know that. But are you sure you want to go?'

'Of course I'm sure. What else is there for me now? And anyhow you said you'd like it.'

'I know I did. But I'll miss the Operatic. They rang up at lunch time to ask me to play the lead in the Christmas show. It's *Carousel*. And no audition either.'

'Kath, what did you tell them?' He sounded nervous.

She smiled. 'What do you think I told them?'

He tried to smile too. 'It would be a lot worse staying here. For me I mean.'

'I know that, you silly.' All of a sudden she felt sorry for him. 'Cup of tea, Walt?'

'I don't mind. I could do with one I mean.'

She filled the kettle. 'Tell me more about the inquiry.'

'There's nothing to tell. Except that old Williams hates my guts.'

'Are you surprised?'

'No. But he needn't have said what he did.'

'What did he say?'

'That I'd done it on purpose. Mind you the chairman told him off for saying it.'

'Any hope they'll get her off?'

'Not the way she's lying.'

'What about Armstrong?'

'The Superintendent? Oh, he was all right. He's neutral anyway. All he said was that I'm not a boozer. Otherwise he just sits there and keeps his mouth shut. Not like all those other bastards.'

'Isn't he a friend of Williams?'

'Said to be. Only because they were Blue Funnel apprentices together.'

'Will Williams get another ship?'

'He might if they had one. But they haven't. Everyone knows that.'

'I'm sorry for him.'

'I might be too if he hadn't said what he did.'

'Walt, you can't altogether blame him for thinking it. After all you've lost him his ship.'

'It's time he retired anyhow. He must be sixty and he's just an old womanizer.'

'Will the Company look after him?'

'I suppose so. Their pension fund's all right.'

'When shall we tell Margaret?'

'Tell Margaret what?'

'That we're leaving here.'

'Not yet. There's time enough for that.'

'Oh, Walt dear, I *wish* it hadn't happened!'

'So do I – now. But it has. And that's it.'

'Yes, dear, but – oh, here she is!'

Bursting gaily into the kitchen, Margaret dropped her satchel on the lino. She was a child of nine now, tall and big-boned like her mother.

'Been good today?' her father asked.

Margaret nodded. She had bright eyes and brighter cheeks. 'Daddy, what do you think? In geography this morning Miss Summers was talking about the Channel Islands and I told her we're going to live there. In Jersey, isn't it?'

'How the devil do you know that?'

Margaret, dancing on the lino, laughed. 'I heard Mummy and you talking after I'd gone to bed on Sunday and you thought I was asleep. But I wasn't. Daddy, Miss Summers says people speak French in Jersey and everyone can eat new potatoes instead of old ones. And tomatoes too. Only I don't like tomatoes ... And Daddy, after the class Miss Summers said she'll be sorry to lose me and asked why we were going. So I told her.'

'Told her what?'

'That because of that accident to some ship you were bloody well finished with being a pilot, I heard you telling Mummy that too. Only of course I didn't tell Miss Summers you used the naughty word "bloody".'

'What did she say then?'

'Nothing much. Only that she'd read all about it and quite understood.'

On the day of the Pilotage Committee inquiry Sir Henry also went straight home. He was driven from the office by his chauffeur, and during the half-hour journey he did not, as was his custom, read any of the papers in his office bag, a fine one once made in London from the skin of a New Guinea crocodile and likely to remain serviceable for many years to come. Instead he dozed and thought, and dozed.

His wife was sewing in the smaller drawing-room. As usual she had changed into a dinner frock, and as she glanced up it struck him not for the first time how much more discontented she now looked than when she had married him. He wondered if it was entirely his fault. It was not, he decided, as they kissed without feeling.

'Before you get a drink tell me if you've thought any more about Jamaica,' she began with eagerness, pushing aside the *petit point* square on which she had been working for the past two years. 'Anne rang up again saying she and Robert are definitely going and how nice it would be if we could overlap.'

Sir Henry could not help frowning. 'I'm afraid I haven't given it another thought. With all this trouble you'll have to go without me. It'll be weeks before everything's cleared up.'

Lady Hartley pouted. 'But surely you'll be clear by November?'

'I wish I could think so.'

The glossy telephone on the antique piecrust table rang, and she hurried to it. 'It's Anne, I expect, I told her I'd ask you the moment you came home ... Oh no, it's only the office for you.'

He took the receiver from her ring-encrusted fingers.

'Sir Henry here ... Oh, it's you Beecher. What is it now?' He listened without speaking. 'Good night,' he said at last, replacing the receiver. He moved across the room and poured out a whisky and soda. Decanters and bottles stood on a side table under a Lely portrait of someone else's ancestor. 'A gin for you, Diana?'

She nodded. 'Yes, it seems to have been a horrid day for me too.'

'Doing what?'

She no longer hunted but he knew the answer. A ride round the farm, a coffee morning or a Conservative sale of work, lunch with Sally or Clare or some other of her friends, a bridge four somewhere in the afternoon or a Women's Institute meeting, and perhaps yet another argument with the competent elderly housekeeper – his chauffeur's wife – or the equally competent but cantankerous head gardener.

She told him, but clearly she was still thinking about Jamaica. 'What did the office want?' she asked absently.

'Beecher says there's a gale warning for tonight and he's had to withdraw the craft and men working to lighten the *Samarai*.'

'Is that very bad?'

'Of course it's bad. She's still full of cargo and in the position she's lying she's likely to break her back.'

'Break her back? I don't quite understand.'

'Split in the middle, my dear. And sink in two useless halves.' Sir Henry wondered why so many women who look intelligent are not.

'Has the insurance money been paid yet?'

'No. So far I haven't abandoned the ship, and until I do she's not officially a total loss.'

She sipped her gin. 'What worries you poor men have over things like this. Didn't you say the pilotage inquiry was today?'

54

'I did.'

'What have they done to that wretched pilot?'

'I haven't yet heard.'

'How you must hate him. I know I do, spoiling the whole autumn like this.'

Sir Henry drank the rest of his whisky and soda in a gulp. 'As a matter of fact I don't,' he replied. 'I don't hate anyone nowadays. Not even myself.'

CHAPTER V

1

The New Guinea Steamship Company held its own inquiry twenty-four hours after the Pilotage Committee's. It took place behind closed doors in the company's boardroom and was conducted by Captain Beecher, the company's one-time Commodore or senior captain and now its marine superintendent. Though the inquiry was private the news somehow leaked that Captain Williams and the Third Officer were exonerated from blame, also that the quartermaster came in for criticism but was exonerated too. Mr Gosling attended to give evidence, and those pausing for a few seconds outside the boardroom door claimed to have heard voices raised in anger – voices variously identified as those of Captain Beecher, Captain Williams, and the quartermaster.

Its proceedings lasted for just over an hour; as soon as they were over Captain Beecher was seen to leave the boardroom and enter Sir Henry's private suite of rooms. He reappeared after five minutes to send in Captain Williams, who remained inside for fifteen. Mr Gosling was sent in next; it was presumed he handed in his resignation or was dismissed – not that either step was necessary since as a Third Class pilot he was no longer permitted to handle vessels as large as those of the New Guinea Company. Later in the afternoon Captain Beecher was known to have telephoned to the Superintendent of Pilotage about appropriated pilots and the name of another First Class pilot was put forward. But with the loss of the *Samarai* together with the sale of the *Kakoda* earlier in the year it seemed doubtful if the company would now have sufficient sailings to justify an appropriation.

As for the *Samarai*, the expected gale did not mature and the work of unloading her cargo into lighters went on uninterrupted for a further week. But the gale which then blew up, a north-wester and a real snorter, lasted for fourteen hours, reaching Force 8 and at its peak Force 10. It was then the vessel's back was broken. The forward half slid into sand clear of the Revetment; the afterpart fell back into the Channel and constituted so serious a danger to navigation that it had to be removed by divers using explosives, a tedious and lengthy task which Captain Coldstream saw through with his usual skill. The operation cost the Dockboard over £100,000 which they were unable to recover from the company or from anyone else because by then the ship had been legally abandoned, and the amount ultimately received by the sale of scrap and fittings did not exceed £10,000. For the record, eight months passed before the wreck buoys were removed and the Channel was declared clear.

Immediately after the *Samarai* broke her back and was abandoned Sir Henry requested his insurance brokers, a Liverpool firm of repute, to lodge his claims. The hull was insured for £760,000, disbursements for £35,000 – 'disbursements' include such items as fuel oil and victuals aboard, port dues paid out during the earlier stages of the voyage, and such like. Of the total of £795,000 approximately one third had been placed on the Liverpool market among nine different marine insurance companies; as is customary the remainder had been taken by the London market. No single Liverpool company had written more than £35,000 – some had written less – but even so it was a heavy enough loss to make certain underwriting accounts look sick.

Anyone who has succeeded in getting a few pounds out of British Railways as recompense for lost or damaged goods is well aware of the lapse of time which usually occurs between the rendering of the claim and the day when it is actually paid. In the marine insurance world there are no such delays. But many different interests are often involved when the sum insured is large, and some of them may be continental. Hence Sir Henry, though knowing a settlement was on the way, did not expect to receive his cheque for another week or two.

At the weekly meeting in the Underwriters' Room, situated in a building on Exchange Flags, it was proposed by the leader's claims assessor and agreed by all other claims assessors present that the New Guinea Steamship Company's hull insurance rates should be increased on annual renewal. At the same time all felt there was little chance of the loss being recovered, seeing it was common knowledge that the company's trade was declining and in consequence Sir Henry was unlikely to renew his fleet or even replace the *Samarai*.

And there the unhappy affair might have ended, because somewhere in the world a ship is lost each day and no marine insurance company could continue to show profits and sometimes losses on its underwriting account – or indeed exist at all – if means were found to abolish every peril of the sea.

2

Dockland is as warm a spawning-ground for rumour as the army during wartime, and long before the gulls had taken possession of the mast and bridge on the stranded forepart of the *Samarai* people were beginning to talk.

Notwithstanding Mr Rowley's assurance to witnesses that anything said at the inquiry would remain within the committee room's four walls, the substance of Captain Williams' outburst, albeit in a distorted form, was known outside, and throughout the south-end docks it was already being said that the pilot had put his ship on the Revetment deliberately. No one quite knew why, but of the various reasons put forward one fulfilled the ever-present need for sex by whispering that Sir Henry had been after the pilot's wife. That she happened to be an amateur actress, even if of only local renown, added credence.

With or without reason the rumour spread. By the time it had run through the north-end docks and crossed the river to Birkenhead it had reached the ears of two of the marine insurance companies, and for what it was worth the general manager of one reported it to his board. It was pooh-poohed by those of his directors who knew Sir Henry. But at the end of the board meeting its chairman, button-holing the general manager and speaking privately to him, said he would raise no objection if the matter was placed in the hands of inquiry agents, provided the fee was shared with the other Liverpool marine companies involved.

When money is at stake men clutch at straws, and after confidential discussions in the basement chamber of the Underwriters' Room it was agreed to call in a high-class London firm.

These Londoners were at least fast workers and their ultimate report, part of it garnered from dockside pubs and elsewhere by their staff of retired detective officers and the like, was not entirely of negative value. It first mentioned what well-informed shipping circles already knew – that Sir Henry owed a substantial sum to a consortium of finance houses and merchant banks, insurance companies too, which had combined to advance in the form of a mortgage sufficient cash to have enabled the New Guinea Steamship Company to order and pay for the *Samarai*. It also disclosed that the pilot had recently acquired a residence in the Channel Islands, the inference being that he was possibly contemplating early retirement from the pilotage service. Of greater significance – at least to the snoopers and their clients – was the revelation that the pilot's wife was Sir Henry's niece by his first marriage. This, as the report pointed out, effectively nailed down and scotched the most salacious of the rumours. But what the report did not point out was that the relationship, though no doubt now forgotten by most of the few outsiders originally aware of it, was still generally known in the circle in which the Goslings moved, also to some in Sir Henry's office. Moreover at no time had Sir Henry wished or attempted to conceal it.

The report added that Captain Williams had been duly interviewed and that it was disappointing to have to state that he admitted his allegation had been made in the heat of the moment and was based entirely on suspicion and not on evidence.

In short there was nothing to enable the insurance companies to throw out the claim. One or two hot-heads, it is believed, initially thought otherwise. But cooler counsels prevailed, largely because insurance companies refrain from washing their dirty linen in the law courts unless assured of unqualified victory.

CHAPTER VI

1

Elderly though Captain Williams was now becoming and whatever may have been his conduct in earlier life, it would be very wrong to stigmatize him in Gosling's scornful words to his wife as 'an old womanizer'. A victim of his own life history, it can more fairly and correctly be said of him that though still recognized as a fine seaman he had developed too many kinks to be rated by his colleagues and acquaintances as an agreeable companion.

The son of a Welsh-speaking farmer in North Wales, his youthful ambition and determination to go to sea rather than work on the family's mountainous land had proved just sufficient to weigh the scales in his favour during the interview which followed his application to become an apprentice in the Blue Funnel line. His apprenticeship lasted three years. He was reported 'very good' in navigation, seamanship, and kindred subjects; in character he was described as reliable, dour, and inclined to be self-opinionated. It was not the practice of Blue Funnel to keep their apprentices; all, even the best among them, were sent away and told if they wished they could apply to return once they had obtained their Extra Master's ticket elsewhere. Hence every Blue Funnel officer holds high qualifications, not the only reason why among sea-going folk Blue Funnel's reputation is un-rivalled throughout the world.

Ifor Williams was one of those who did not return to Blue Funnel. When his apprenticeship ended he became a probationary Fourth Officer in the New Guinea Steamship Company, and due to its growing fleet he was quickly promoted to Third Officer, then to Second. As two youngsters on the New Guinea coast he and Henry Hartley naturally became acquainted; each appreciated and understood the other's direct and sometimes ruthless methods of getting things done.

Williams had married while a Second Officer. His marriage – to a Cardiff woman who admitted to having been a prostitute – was disastrous and did not last a year; they had separated by mutual consent and thereafter neither knew nor cared whether the other was still alive. Because of his strict Calvinistic upbringing there had been no divorce. In any event he had no wish to marry again: at that time he preferred his women where he could find them.

Partly because of his broken marriage and partly for other reasons, Williams had been content to remain with the New Guinea Steamship Company. Promotion was speedier than in many other companies and security seemed as great: he liked the trade and the long duration of the round-voyages – three months at the very least – and he liked New Guinea and the various races who lived there. Indeed he had better friends in New Guinea than in England or in Wales. His OBE, won during the second war, was awarded for superb seamanship in saving the *Sariba* after a torpedo struck her in Atlantic convoy.

He was now a fit man just turned sixty and his tastes were simple. While Merseyside was still being bombed he had bought a house very cheaply in Egerton Park, a curious and secluded backwater once on the fringe of Rock Ferry's countryside. As though to remind strangers of its better days it is still approached through entrance gateways, one at either end and flanked by tall stone pillars. Facing its ill-kept private roadway several dozen houses were built perhaps seventy years earlier in Victorian designs of varying ugliness. Many, detached and semi-detached alike, had quite large gardens. Egerton Park, when Williams first went to live there, was thus shabby and unexpected yet somehow charming. Of recent years it has suffered rehabilitation at the hands of builders who have pulled down half its original houses, though Williams's still remains. Villas and bungalows of the type beloved by present-day architects replace them. Many of the gardens have gone too, land in Rock Ferry being nowadays much too valuable for anything as unprofitable as grass and shrubs and old trees.

Captain Williams did not remain on his own for long. Hearing of a housekeeper, a youngish Birkenhead warwidow, he installed her in his house as Mrs Williams, and they lived together as man and wife during his brief periods ashore.

As a foundation member of the *Landfall* – a Tank landing-craft acquired from the Admiralty after the war, converted into a floating club for Merchant Navy officers and others, and moored alongside the quay of Canning Dock a few cables distant from the Pier Head – he lunched aboard whenever possible and sometimes went there for an hour or two in the evenings to escape from Mrs Williams. At heart he was not a landsman. His life was too deeply rooted in the sea and he had not contemplated the retirement which the loss of the *Samarai* so suddenly enforced. Nor had he saved enough to view the prospect with equanimity. Thus from being a capable and reasonably contented if crusty sea-captain he had turned into a man with a bitter grievance. For that reason the sole result – to him – of the interview he had unwillingly granted to the representative of the London firm of private investigators was to plant in his mind the tiny seed of a dangerous but brilliant idea.

The interview, by appointment of course, took place in Williams's house. It soon became clear that the interviewer, a retired detective inspector from the Birmingham area, knew nothing of the sea or of its ways. Furthermore he was giving nothing away. But Williams guessed from his questions that some kind of conspiracy was now suspected, and since he suspected the same thing himself the two men got on well with one another. Williams was unable to say anything more than he had already told the Pilotage Committee; in fact in answer to a direct question he had to admit he had no evidence whatsoever of the pilot having grounded his ship on purpose. It was merely a hunch, he told his interviewer, adding that as often as not his hunches came close to the truth. After half an hour of question and answer the ex-detective departed with several fingers of whisky – illegally salved from the *Samarai*'s bonded store – inside him, and Williams found himself left with an idea which began to grow every bit as quickly and strongly as Jack's bean seed of the fairy tale.

Its growth was encouraged by a domestic upheaval which had occurred on the morning of that same day. Mrs Williams, not at the best of times a sweet-tempered woman, had been more and more put out by her man's increasing surliness. For his part Captain Williams, always a poor sleeper when ashore, had been enduring a succession of nearly sleepless nights due to his grievance and to increasing worries about the economic uncertainty of his future. Even so there was little excuse for such bad language over the under-boiling of his breakfast egg.

Mrs Williams still had a good figure but since their unofficial marriage the lines on her face had hardened and the blondness of her hair was no longer natural.

'You're nothing better than a nasty old stoat with a sore head,' she told him succinctly. 'You being ashore for life is too bloody much for me and what's more I'm not taking it one day longer. In other words I'm off.'

In all the circumstances her announcement came almost as a relief, and he had not argued with her. She'd done the same sort of thing once or twice before, he remembered, but she'd always come back. On this occasion he wasn't even asking her where she was going or to whom. Probably, he thought, to that Bromborough motor salesman chap separated from his wife, she'd talked enough about the big red Jaguar he drove about in. Or it might be to her cousin the master butcher in Chester, at least she'd always said he was her cousin. But whoever it was he wasn't giving her the satisfaction of inquiring, he'd just show her he couldn't care less. So all he did was to offer to drive her to the station in Rock Ferry, an offer she refused. After breakfast he'd heard her telephoning for a taxi, and she'd gone all right.

The following morning, strange to say, he awoke refreshed, pleasantly conscious of having slept for five or six hours and alert from the moment he opened his eyes. Best of all he now knew exactly what to do. Clearly others were thinking as he thought – why else should the big insurance companies take the unusual step of bringing in private inquiry agents? The man they had sent to interview him had shown he was out of his depth in a crime of the sea such as this ... Who indeed was better placed and equipped than himself to bring about Sir Henry's downfall? And as the principal sufferer was it not his right too? ... Though not a religious man it was as if the Calvinistic streak inherited from his forbears had suddenly manifested itself, and he saw himself appointed as the instrument of God ... Justice, not revenge, was all he wanted, and he sought no material reward. Perhaps that is why the thought never entered his head that in every respect except that of intent the course of action he had decided upon could only be described as criminal.

Filled with increasing enthusiasm he got up, shaved with care, and dressed. He was a tidy-minded man, and after breakfast he cleaned up in the kitchen and left everything shipshape. No need to think about lunch, the *Landfall* would provide that. And after lunch his first port of call would be Sir Henry, the second, Mr Gosling. But before setting off for Liverpool it would be necessary to rehearse what he intended to say to each one of them, and this he did to his complete satisfaction while walking twice round the perimeter of the private roadway which served the houses and gardens of Egerton Park. He also made sure that a certain sheet of paper was still safely in the breast pocket of his best jacket.

Finally leaving home at twelve o'clock he travelled to Liverpool by the Mersey Railway from Rock Ferry and went straight to the *Landfall*. There, after drinking a pint of beer by himself at the bar, he sat down for lunch at the table where Captain Armstrong of the pilotage was already sitting. Others at the same table included the junior of the Dockboard's several Harbour Masters and two shipping executives who kept good friends though they came from rival offices. Of recent weeks Williams had rarely been seen on the *Landfall* and it is doubtful if his presence that day was welcome. Since the loss of his ship he seemed unable to talk about anything else and he was fast becoming one of the club's bores.

But throughout lunch he did not once mention the *Samarai*: indeed he was so self-contained and silent that Captain Armstrong, beside whom he was sitting, felt constrained to ask if he was all right. Williams replied cheerfully enough that he was, and then he asked Arm-

66

strong if Gosling had settled down yet as a Third Class pilot. Armstrong replied 'So far as I know he has,' and Williams then asked if Gosling was working that afternoon. Armstrong answered he didn't know and if Williams really wanted to know he'd better ask the Shoremaster.

Captain Armstrong, on the point of leaving his table to return to his office, did not prolong the conversation, though later he was able to recall that Williams's interest in Gosling had struck him as somewhat strange.

Captain Williams left the *Landfall* shortly after two and went to the New Guinea Steamship Company's offices in Water Street where he told Sir Henry's secretary, Miss Webb, that he wished for a few words in private with Sir Henry on his return from lunch. Miss Webb replied that Sir Henry was catching a train to London later in the afternoon and could Captain Williams therefore call some other day? Williams replied the matter was pressing and that he would not keep Sir Henry for more than a very few minutes, and Miss Webb, who had always liked Williams and now felt sorry for him, said she would see what she could arrange and in the meantime would he please wait in the Captains' Room? She asked finally if she could inform Sir Henry of the subject about which he wished to speak to him, and Williams replied, 'Just my pension.'

Twenty minutes later Williams received his summons by internal telephone, and Miss Webb conducted him into Sir Henry's inner room. Immediately afterwards she logged the time of his entry, as she did with all visitors. She logged names and departure times too; this particular interview lasted eleven minutes.

Sir Henry and Captain Williams were almost contemporaries, and though each had known the other for more than thirty years and though each in his own way had climbed the company's ladder of success they had not thereby become friends. Their relationship now was no more and no less than that which usually prevails between shipowner and senior captain, that is to say cordial but remote, though it is probable Sir Henry held Williams in respect. On the other hand Williams held Sir Henry in no respect at all, either then or previously, and any psychoanalyst, had Williams ever contemplated going to one, would have diagnosed the cause as deep-seated jealousy.

Sir Henry was seated at his broad, flat-topped desk. He motioned Williams to sit beside him in the leather-covered chair with the big arms. 'Light your pipe if you want, I know it's useless offering you a cigarette,' he said. 'What can I do for you, Williams?'

'It is about my pension I have come to see you, sir.'

'So Miss Webb has told me. But I thought all that was settled a couple of weeks ago?'

'At the time I thought it too, sir. But on reading the Company's big pension book more studiously I am thinking Section II 4 (c) applies in my favour.'

The rules of the Company's pension fund had, like the fund itself, grown considerably during recent decades, and, like those of many another pension scheme, had perhaps become over-complicated – in the New Guinea Company's case a whole section with various small-type amendments was devoted solely to its coloured or native employees. The point now raised by Captain Williams referred specifically to the cause of his retirement, being due neither to age nor ill-health nor to involuntary change of place of residence. Nor was it, strictly speaking, a case of redundancy.

Sir Henry grasped the issue at once. He too felt a good deal of sympathy for his unlucky captain, and though pressed for time that afternoon he concealed it. 'You must realize I'm only one of several trustees but on the face of it you appear to have quite a case for upgrading. In fact under the provisions of Section V I believe you could even be said to qualify for receiving, ex gratia of course, an additional annual payment. Leave it with me, Williams, and I'll speak to its managers. Off the record I think you can safely rely on a reasonable increase. Would a further couple of hundred a year satisfy you?'

'Indeed it would,' Williams replied with a sincerity he was quite unable to control.

There were air-travel tickets on Sir Henry's desk, he now noticed, and next his eye caught a glimpse of Sir Henry's pigskin suitcase on the far table beside his black hat and overcoat. 'I must not detain you another moment, Sir Henry. I know you are a busy man, busier than me unfortunately.'

Sir Henry smiled. 'Between you and me I admit for a man of my age and health I'm kept much too busy.'

The interview ended thus informally, and on the way out Williams made it his business to exchange a pleasantry or two with Miss Webb. 'Keeping quite well, I hope?' he began.

'Yes, thanks. And you?'

'I must not complain.'

'Completed your business with Sir Henry to your satisfaction?'

'Yes indeed. And I see he is off on his travels again. How far is he going this time?'

'Only to London and the continent.'

'I am old-fashioned and do not take kindly to aeroplane-travel myself. If he leaves this afternoon I am very fortunate to have seen him.'

Expert in ridding herself of the unwanted, Miss Webb

raised her eyes to the clock on the wall. 'Excuse me, Captain, I must go to him now, his car's coming in half an hour. So nice to have seen you, take care of yourself.'

2

The dulcet chimes of the electric door bell sounded loud and clear while Mrs Gosling was peeling potatoes in the kitchen and her husband was cleaning his shoes beside her.

'I'll go,' he said in irritation. 'Who the hell can it be at a time like this?'

When he saw who was there he felt too astonished to speak.

'Yes, it is me, Mr Gosling. I have come to bury the hatchet and I would like to talk to you in private.'

Even more astonished Gosling asked, 'What about?'

'I have been to Sir Henry and now I know the truth about the loss of my ship.'

'What are you talking about?'

'You will know soon enough when I tell you I went to Sir Henry because one of the two members of my crew on the bridge beside you was more observant than the other, and from him I have learned something which was not made known to the gentlemen of the Pilotage Committee. You made a slip, Mr Gosling.'

A conversation of this kind taking place on the doorstep is always liable to instant termination by the door being slammed in one's face, and Williams was delighted to see beads of sweat welling up on Gosling's forehead – incidentally caused by anger and not alarm. Nor did it strike him the initial success his shock tactics had undoubtedly scored was due to the sheer improbability of his visit having caught the pilot momentarily off his guard.

For Gosling had now been living long enough with his knowledge of the final events on the bridge of the *Samarai* to feel reasonably secure, and he had found further security in the very fact that he had been adjudged guilty of nothing worse than an error of judgment, for which the penalty had been paid by the punishment he had been awarded. That to him had ended the matter, and in his resilient mind he had already worked out the shape of life to come in Jersey. And now this crazy old man of whom he thought nothing turned up out of the blue, blethering away about knowing something which could put the whole future, his wife's and daughter's too, in jeopardy. This slip just mentioned, what the hell could it be? ... It was essential to find out, and for that and no other reason he stepped clear of the doorway and muttered in a voice too low to be overheard by his wife, 'You're talking arrant bloody nonsense but you'd better come in and say whatever you've come to say inside and not here.'

Accepting the invitation in silence and as his due, Williams followed him into a room on the right, and as soon as the door was closed Gosling said, 'What slip?'

'Not quite so quickly, please. First let me ask you where is your pipe today?'

*   *   *

To Captain Williams this second interview was even more satisfying than the first. All he had come to say had been said, he had correctly predicted most of Gosling's reactions, and he was ready for what he guessed would be the pilot's next move. Everything was going according to plan, and he felt so pleased with himself that though he had refused the drink ultimately offered to him – on the grounds that he never took spirits in the afternoons – he called at the *Landfall* on his way home for a double brandy. The time of day was such that only one other member was present, and he was deaf. But that did not matter; all the company Williams needed was provided by his soaring thoughts.

CHAPTER VII

(October 18 & 19)

1

Dockboard members are provided with a free lunch only on board days and on such other days as the committees on which they serve may be sitting, and one morning shortly after the *Samarai*'s final death throes Mr Arthur Bernard found himself compelled to lunch at his club. The club was a small one tucked away in an old-fashioned building behind the then equally old-fashioned Bank of England building in Castle Street, one of its lesser attractions being that from its staircase window members could see Bank of England girls in a back room counting old bank-notes by the thousand.

On entering the smokeroom he spotted Malcolm McGregor, general manager of the Trident, the marine insurance branch of the Royal and Ancient Assurance, and they sat down to drink their glass of sherry together.

Bernard said, 'Cheers ... Did you see the poor old *Samarai* has broken her back?'

Malcolm McGregor, fed up to the back teeth with the *Samarai* and everything connected with her, winced and said, 'I did see it.'

'We heard the full story at the Pilotage Committee. It sounded fishy to me.'

McGregor, regretting the glass of sherry which temporarily bound them together, said, 'Did it?'

Bernard, who did not know the marine insurance companies had lain on their own inquiry and that the

73

report which had reached the Trident that very morning was hardly worth a pound note, nodded and continued, 'I told them so too.'

'What was fishy?'

'Nothing very specific. But I'm sure it was. There were fireworks at the inquiry, believe me.'

'I do believe you.' McGregor finished his sherry in a hurry and said, 'Arthur, I'm leaving you. I want to lunch early today.'

Arthur Bernard fired his parting shot. 'Malcolm, old boy, if I were running your insurance company I don't mind telling you I wouldn't pay up too quickly.'

Malcolm McGregor did not reply, and on his way up the staircase to the luncheon room his thoughts were grim. It riled him that the inquiry had proved abortive; the thirty-odd thousand his company was going to lose riled him more. And now a member of the Dockboard, one not quite so dim as some of them and who'd also been present at the pilotage investigation, had as good as told him he didn't know his business ... A piece of infernal cheek, yet one which might well be true. For during that well-remembered and controversial meeting in the Underwriters' Room the other day hadn't he told Fred Goring of the Dolphin and that obstinate mule George Brown of Neptune he felt convinced they were settling with indecent haste?

Results are what count in the present-day world, never mind by what route they are reached, and as Malcolm McGregor entered the luncheon room and before studying the menu he had made a decision which was to enhance his reputation for prescience – Arthur Bernard's too – thus proving, as if often suspected, that in big business the destinies and very lives of others are liable to be governed by chance encounters and capricious conversations between friends.

74

On returning to his office after lunch Mr McGregor summoned Mr Martin, his claims assessor, and told him to speak to the CID.

'About what, sir, may I ask?'

'The *Samarai* of course. Let them have all our files and the inquiry report so that they can see we weren't satisfied but can't prove a thing. And if they're prepared to take it on tell all the other companies what we've done, it doesn't matter whether they're with us or not ... But leave the Neptune to me, I'll tell Brown myself.'

Mr Martin was so delighted that for once he smiled. 'Very well, Mr McGregor, I'll get moving at once.' He too was grieved that the Trident was parting with such a whack with no prospect of getting it back in increased premiums, and to him the aphorism about insurance companies *liking* to pay claims had always seemed old hat.

2

A male voice at Divisional Headquarters asked Mr Martin if it could help him, and Mr Martin said it could and explained he had a matter in connection with an insurance claim which his management wished him to discuss with the appropriate police officer.

'I'll put you through to Detective Chief Inspector Young, sir,' the voice said.

In telling his wife about it that evening Mr Martin said what impressed him most was the speed and courtesy of the police, Chief Inspector Young saying he'd be with him inside twenty minutes and not to go to the trouble of bringing round the papers himself.

The chief inspector knew how to listen, and when Mr Martin had told his story and was saying diffidently that his general manager was wondering if this was quite the kind of matter the police would be prepared to investigate, Young assured him it was. 'May I take away the papers and study them more closely than I can here?' he inquired.

'With pleasure,' Mr Martin replied.

'How soon do you want them back?'

Mr Martin, an occasional reader of detective fiction, permitted himself one of his rare mild jests. 'You may retain them till the case has been solved and the criminal brought to justice.'

Departing from the offices of the Trident, Detective Chief Inspector Young crossed Exchange Flags with the bundle of *Samarai* papers under his arm. This could be interesting, he thought as he lit his pipe and recalled the dockland talk which had come to his ears soon after the grounding. Then, having other and more pressing affairs on his mind, he dismissed this new one till several hours later when, having put on his slippers, he pulled his armchair nearer the fire, polished his spectacles, untied the tape, and began to read.

Like most chief inspectors in the CID Young had to take work home with him. Not that he minded or expected otherwise – he was a dedicated policeman. He owed his rank to good health, experience, personality, fortitude, and sound common sense. He himself would have claimed none of these virtues; had he been asked he would have attributed his present position to seniority, retirement of others, and luck – the luck of having been in the right place at the right time on a number of occasions during the past twenty-five years. In this at least he was at one with Sir Henry.

Tying up the papers nearly an hour later, he called to his wife he was now ready for supper. He had made a few notes and had sifted his thoughts. I'll put Richardson on to this, it's right up his street and as there aren't so many to question he'll soon see its shape. But I do wish he'd been in the navy and not the air force, there's a ship involved in this and he won't know the language ...

At the office next morning he summoned Richardson, the junior detective inspector of the Division. Recently promoted from sergeant – a good promotion too in the opinion of the ranks of Y Division – Inspector Richardson was a middle-aged man of athletic build whose curly hair, once brown, was now grey and wearing a bit thin. The strong cut of his jaw belied the usual geniality of his blue eyes. He had been a fighter-pilot during the war; at the age of thirty he had married a red-haired policewoman and their young son Charles, having red hair too, answered to the name of Copper.

'What are you on with now, Bob?' Chief Inspector Young asked him.

'The Brassey Street queer who got a knife in his back, sir.'

'Know who did it?'

'Not yet, sir.'

'Hand it over to Harry Parker. I've something less sordid for you here.'

'I can do with it,' Richardson said with a grin.

'Heard of the *Samarai*?' Young adjusted his spectacles.

'Of course.'

'One of the insurance companies concerned thinks it wasn't an accident.'

'Have they much to go on?'

'Hardly a thing.' Young opened his drawer. 'Only this. Catch.'

Richardson caught the heavy bundle. 'Hell, all these?'

'There's less in them than you'd think. Seems the

77

insurance companies smelled a rat and called in inquiry agents. You'll find their report at the top – they didn't get far but I've marked a few things for you to follow up. From our point of view there's not much in the rest, only that between them the companies have to part with three-quarters of a million and they don't like it. You'll see some of their private squeals too, I've put them at the bottom ... Bob, there's big money in shipping. You and I are in the wrong job.'

'So I've been thinking for a long time, sir.'

'When can you start?'

'Today if I break my appointment with the licensee of the Brassey Street pub. I'll tell Harry Parker I reckon he knows more than he's letting on.'

Young nodded. 'Two or three more things before you go. First about the *Samarai* herself. There's a bit of hearsay in the inquiry agents' report which doesn't add up to much – the captain blaming the pilot, as of course he would. Learn what actually happened to cause her to go on the Revetment, the pilotage office of the Dockboard will know that. They hold their own inquiries whenever a ship has an accident and one of their pilots is involved. I know Armstrong the pilotage Superintendent, he's a sound chap and won't confuse you with nautical language if you tell him you're not familiar with it. And learn what you can about how and why the pilot's bought a house in the Channel Islands, also if there's anything significant in his wife being Hartley's niece. And don't forget the Company itself could be in financial difficulties. I think that's all for now, Bob. Get on with it and let me know should you find you need anyone to help you.'

CHAPTER VIII

(October 19)

1

That morning about noon Inspector Richardson left the Divisional office and walked swiftly along Dale Street towards the Pier Head. Having read through the *Samarai* papers he had decided to interview the Superintendent of pilotage first.

He nodded to a Y Division sergeant on special duty outside the Town Hall where some minor royalty was expected for lunch, and by turning left at the bottom of Water Street for Canning Dock he reached and entered the pilotage office.

On days when his committee was not sitting Captain Armstrong, not usually in uniform, used the committee room as his office, and he rose when Richardson entered and asked what he could do for him.

Richardson explained, and Armstrong said, 'When you phoned for an appointment I thought that might be why you were coming. We do have a report of all our inquiries and in them we record the evidence of each witness, though not in his actual words. I'm not entitled to show you the *Samarai* report but I have my chairman's permission to tell you what I can, and I think you'll learn all you want if I get out the chart and show you what happened and how the Pilotage Committee understood the casualty to have occurred.'

'Thanks, I'd like that.'

Armstrong spread out the chart on the big table,

demonstrated with his pencil the course of the *Samarai* along Crosby Channel, and went on to explain who was on the bridge and what orders were given and by whom up to the moment of grounding. He then looked at Richardson and said, 'If I'm not speaking out of turn I suppose you're inquiring because there's now some suspicion this wasn't an accident.'

'Well, that could be so.'

Rolling up the chart, the Superintendent said, 'I've had the same thought myself.'

'In that case can you tell me anything which might help me?'

Captain Armstrong thought for a moment and said, 'A little, perhaps. Though it doesn't amount to a lot. Williams the *Samarai*'s captain happens to be one of my oldest friends – we met first as youngsters – but remember I'm the Superintendent here and have to be guarded in what I say about my pilots. Remember too that pilots are judged by the Committee and not by me.'

'I understand all that. Let's begin with the pilot. What can you tell me about him?'

'This much. Most shipowners consult me before choosing their appropriated pilot. Sir Henry Hartley did so, and I told him what I still believe to be the truth about Mr Gosling – that he's a very good pilot and a steady man in every way except one. I warned Sir Henry he was known to be a gambler.'

Richardson laughed. 'Aren't we all?'

'Gosling went in for it in a much heavier way than most. From time to time I heard he was in financial difficulties.' Here Captain Armstrong gave a faint smile. 'You see in the pilotage service there aren't many secrets. In the pilot boats men live very close together, often for a number of days at a time.'

'What's his particular kind of gambling? Dogs? The stock market? Or horses?'

'Horses, I understand. Anyhow Sir Henry took him and made it clear to me the fact that Gosling happened to be a relative of his by marriage had nothing to do with it. He said he wanted first and foremost a good pilot, and what a pilot did when not on one of his ships was not his business. I told Sir Henry in that case I thought he was making an excellent choice. I was speaking of Mr Gosling as a pilot of course.'

'What do you mean by that?'

'No more than I have said. I know next to nothing of Mr Gosling's private life.'

'What about Sir Henry Hartley? Do you know him?'

'Hardly at all. I've spoken to him on the telephone, but only very rarely. His marine superintendent Captain Beecher sees me about matters which can't be dealt with by our respective office staffs. So I'm afraid I can't help you there.'

Richardson made a note of Beecher's name in his book and asked, 'Could the quartermaster have had anything to do with the grounding?'

Captain Armstrong shrugged his shoulders. 'Donovan? Most things are possible, but I should say not. At the inquiry he struck me as being an honest but very angry man. He was mainly concerned about his own position.'

'Isn't that to be expected?'

Captain Armstrong shrugged again. 'Certainly, unless he's a good actor. A very good one too, assuming his anger was put on.'

'Could he have been got at? Bribed I mean?'

'Many men are prone to that. In his case I should think it unlikely.'

'You say you've known Captain Williams for a long time. What can you tell me about him?'

'Ifor Williams isn't what you'd call an easy man. But he's an excellent master and thoroughly deserved the OBE he got for saving one of his company's ships during the war. He's impetuous at times, excitable too, but remember he's a Welshman. We were Blue Funnel apprentices together, and after that our ways parted. Somehow we always kept in touch, and when I was appointed here, this being his home port, we resumed our friendship. Or as much of a friendship as one can have with a man of the type of Williams. I suppose his early matrimonial troubles account for his awkwardness – his wife of course was a woman of the streets and the story goes he married her to save her. It's the sort of story I believe too, because he's like that. He's not the sort of man to have intimate friends and I suppose I'm closer to him than anyone else on Merseyside. But being comparatively friendless doesn't seem to worry him – he lives for his job and nothing else and that's why he's taken the loss of his ship so hard. He has a woman living with him now, she came originally as his housekeeper and I suppose it's an arrangement which suits both of them.'

'You know her too?'

'Only slightly. She's lived with him for the last ten or twelve years. She's not at all a bad woman of her kind, a bit quick-tempered perhaps. As a title of convenience she's known as Mrs Williams of course. She's not a clever woman if you know what I mean, but she provides a home for him to come back to. And she's a good cook, which is something these days with all the young women working in shops or offices before they marry.'

'My wife's a grand cook and she was in the police,' Richardson said with a grin. 'You mentioned a relationship by marriage between Gosling and Sir Henry Hartley. What exactly is it?'

'Sir Henry is a self-made man, and I understand his first wife died many years ago. Long before my time here of course. I believe Mrs Gosling is the daughter of her sister. It's to Sir Henry's credit, so people say about him, that when he moved up in the world and remarried he didn't drop any of his first wife's relations.'

'Do you know Mrs Gosling?'

'Again only slightly. I was invited to their wedding because I was the Superintendent. I've seen her perhaps half a dozen times since and heard her at shows once or twice – she's a good singer. But I don't visit them socially if that's what you mean. As Superintendent of all the pilots I can't choose one or two to be on close terms with. If you want my opinion I'd say Mrs Gosling is the stronger character of the two, and though of course there's no blood relationship between her and Sir Henry I've always thought she's got a bit of Sir Henry in her make up.'

'One final question, if I'm not keeping you from your lunch. It seems Gosling has recently bought a house in the Channel Islands, or so we've been told. Do you know anything about that?'

'I had heard of it but I know nothing more than that. A thrifty pilot can become quite well-to-do. I'm not saying Gosling is thrifty, but he may have had his successes on the turf. I'm sorry I can't help you more than that.'

'You've helped me a lot and I'm grateful for all you've told me.'

'If once again I may speak out of turn, I don't think you'll find the answer in what took place aboard the *Samarai*. Ships are wayward things, and she may have taken a sudden turn which caught Gosling on the hop. That's always possible. Anyway whether she did or not, what happened on the bridge and in Crosby Channel was over in a very few seconds. Admittedly Gosling made a mistake, but from all the evidence I've heard no one can prove that when on her bridge he committed anything more than an error of judgment. If indeed it was no accident – and I repeat the "if" – I think you should look for your answer ashore.'

2

Captain Armstrong had given Richardson so much to think about that he returned to Divisional Head-quarters and after lunch read the *Samarai* papers for the second time. Then he compiled a list of every individual connected with the case, however remotely, and after further consideration placed their names in the order in which it seemed best to question them. Thus:

Captain Beecher
Sir Henry Hartley
Donovan, Quartermaster
Livesey, Third Officer
Chief Officer
Gosling
Mrs Gosling
Captain Williams
Mrs Williams
Bank Manager, Hartley's private account
Bank Manager, New Guinea SS Co's account

He spent the following half hour framing and marshalling the questions to be put to each one of them, and on reaching the last two he reluctantly crossed them off the list. He knew by the Bankers' Books Evidence Act, 1879 – which is still in force today – that the first requirement for viewing anyone's bank account was a court order which no magistrate would grant until police proceedings against the person concerned had actually been instituted. A detective is sometimes able to learn what he wants to know by unofficial approach, but not every bank manager will send for a customer's account, leave it face upwards on the table, and vanish from the room for five minutes.

3

There was still time for a further interview that afternoon, and after phoning the New Guinea Steamship Co. Richardson slipped on his mack and went round to India Buildings.

The loss of any fully-laden ship brings its spate of extra work to every department of her owner's office, and Captain Beecher, preoccupied with finding answers to the searching queries contained in yet another letter from that faceless official personage known as the Receiver of Wreck, was far from pleased when told by his telephone exchange that an inspector from the police was on the line asking to come at once and see him. 'What about?' Beecher demanded irritably. 'He says it's about the *Samarai*, sir.' 'Tell him to come if he must.' Beecher was grim now. 'And tell the commissionaire he's to put him in No 2 and on no account to bring him straight to me.'

Though once Commodore or senior captain of the Company's fleet there was nothing of the traditional bluff and hearty sea-dog about Captain Beecher. Thin, tight-lipped, and nowadays bespectacled, he was incorruptible and feared no man – least of all Sir Henry. Thirty years of trading to the Coral Sea had all but destroyed his liver, and the reputation he had earned

85

aboard his ship had accompanied him ashore and still held good – that though sometimes approachable in the afternoons he was always best avoided in the mornings.

So Richardson was kept waiting in No 2 reception room for a good ten minutes, and there was nothing to look at there except a large-scale map of New Guinea on the wall, several out-of-date numbers of *Syren & Shipping*, and a volume entitled *Directory of U.K. Exporters & Importers*.

On steaming into No 2 at last, Captain Beecher gave the impression of wanting to steam out again almost immediately. 'What's all this about?' he asked.

Richardson, not knowing Beecher's scowl was partly due to shortsightedness, told him, and Beecher, who already knew, raised his eyes to heaven – in this case the reception room's low ceiling – and said, 'Hey, yet another inquiry? The Pilotage had one, we had one, I hear the insurance companies had one, and now you come along and say you're having one too. Why can't the poor bloody ship be left to rest in peace now that she's dead and half-buried in sand?'

Richardson sympathized and grinned. 'It's about your own inquiry I've come to see you, sir. I don't want to pry into your Company's affairs but I would like to know its findings.'

'If you don't call that prying, what is? But I'll tell you, young man. We absolved the captain, reprimanded the quartermaster, and sacked the pilot. We had to sack him. Surely you as a detective-inspector know the Pilotage Committee's taken away his First Class licence?'

Richardson quite liked the chap. 'Why did you reprimand the quartermaster, sir?'

'For getting flustered. Otherwise he might have saved the ship.'

'No other reason?'

'Other reason? What other reason? You seem to want to know more than I know myself.'

'I was wondering if you'd any doubts about his integrity. That he might have been got at for instance.'

'That idea hadn't entered my head. Or anyone else's except yours. Donovan's been with the Company nearly as long as I have. And sailed with me for close on twenty years.'

'Excuse me saying that's no reason why someone didn't get at him.'

'I don't excuse you. It so happens I know Donovan and you don't. I know he's hot-headed and got himself logged during this last voyage for some silly incident at Port Moresby. But no one thinks the worse of him for that, I know Williams doesn't. And because he was at the wheel of the *Samarai* and because of all the innuendoes flying about he's now left the sea and taken a shore job. More's the pity too.'

'So in your opinion he's a good man?'

'Of course he's a good man and I'd offer him another ship today if I had one to offer. What are you wanting to pry into next?'

'Can you tell me anything useful about the pilot?'

'Gosling? What do you want me to say about him? That he's a good man too?'

'I understand he's quite a gambler.'

'And looking for money to pay his losses, hey? You'd better ask Sir Henry about that side, he's his uncle by marriage and I'm only the marine super. Who once had nine ships on the run, I don't mind telling you.'

No wonder he's browned off, Richardson was thinking. 'I understand Mr Gosling has hitherto been considered a good pilot. Is that correct?'

'Of course it's correct. Why else d'you think we'd have

employed him? Because of his wife's relationship with the boss? To be fair he *is* a good pilot. Or was till this happened. Which makes it all the more inexplicable. Mind you, she could have taken a sudden sheer – ships are as incalculable as women.'

Richardson rose from the hard waiting-room chair. 'Thanks for all your help, sir. I hope I won't have to trouble you again.'

'So do I.' Then, unexpectedly, Captain Beecher's scowl relaxed into a smile. 'Carry on with the good work and good luck to you ... And if you do come again perhaps I won't keep you waiting so long... Thinking of going in to Sir Henry to quiz him about his nephew's gambling habits?'

'Yes. But not today.'

'That's a good thing. Because he's in Hamburg. Hoping to sell one of our five remaining ships.'

CHAPTER IX

(October 20)

1

Donovan, having lived in Bootle most of his life, had found a job there. He was working in a builder's yard, and next morning Richardson turned up at the address given, timing his arrival for a few minutes before the dinner hour.

Inside the yard a burly middle-aged man was loading bags of cement and bricks into a Bedford truck, and Richardson got out of his car and told him he was looking for Mr Donovan.

'You're looking straight at him now, mister.' Donovan's new cloth cap did not match his florid complexion.

Telling him who he was, Richardson nodded at the truck. 'A bit of a change for you, this, isn't it?'

'It suits me all right.'

'I want a few words with you about the *Samarai*. What about coming out for a drink with me?'

'Suits me too. But I'd best tell the boss who I'm going with and why.'

In the tap-room of the Old Ram's Head in Oriel Road Richardson bought two pints and pointed to a Britannia table in the far corner. 'Over there?' he asked.

'Does for me, mister. And what do you want to know?'

'First of all why you left the New Guinea Steamship Company.'

'They'd nothing else for me. Not enough ships, Captain Beecher said.'

'So you decided to finish with the sea?'

'Ay. After that bloody pilot tried to pin the blame on me what other company would look at a quartermaster with the mud on his back?'

'Why did he try to pin the blame on you?'

'To save his own bloody skin, and that's God's truth.'

'What do you yourself think happened to cause the ship to go aground?'

'Mister, I *know* what happened. She ran aground because the pilot told me to put her there. And that's blunt.'

'Did you say this to the Pilotage Committee?'

'They wouldn't let me. They'd already treated me rough for trying to speak out. And even if they had let me, wouldn't that chairman have come down on me same as he come down on Captain Williams?'

'Don't you now think you made a mistake in not telling them?'

'It wouldn't have made no difference, sir. They didn't want to listen to a quartermaster, they weren't even paying heed to a captain. And them ten judges sitting like owls in a row would never agree together that one of their pilots did a thing like that on purpose. I'd been told that beforehand.'

'Didn't you have the chance of saying it at the Company's own inquiry?'

'What was the use there either? The pilot had already been blamed and punished by the Pilotage and wasn't that enough for the insurance? So Captain Beecher did the same as the Pilotage. And reprimanded me into the bargain.'

'Have you said anything about all this to Captain Williams or the First or Third Officers or to anyone else?'

'I did to Captain Williams after the inquiry in the

company office. I told him what I thought and told him about the pilot fellow fiddling with his pipe after telling me to give her more port. I didn't want to speak to Mr Burton or Mr Livesey. But I may have said something about it in here when I come here in the evenings.'

'During that last voyage of the *Samarai* what were you logged for?' It was a Richardson trick to change the subject suddenly.

Donovan's florid cheeks turned purple. 'I'll not deny it. Excess of zeal was what Captain Williams called it, and all I did was to hit a New Guinea bastard. You'd have done the same as me, sir, he was pissing on the – '

'I'm sure I would and never mind what he was pissing on. Have you a grudge against Captain Williams for logging you?'

'Grudge? *Me*? Not on your life. Things aren't easy in New Guinea now with all the natives thinking they're as well educated as you and me, and Captain Williams only did his duty.'

'Ever been interested in acting, Mr Donovan?'

'Acting? Not likely. The missus and me haven't been inside a theatre for twenty years. And we don't go to the pictures neither.'

Richardson emptied his glass, ordered two more pints, and asked Donovan whether he supported Liverpool or Everton.

'Neither, mister.'

'Neither? How's that?'

And Richardson learned to his surprise that Donovan spent his spare time painting sailing-ships on canvas and on boards. Usually in tropic seas, he said, but sometimes off the Lizard.

'Good morning. Yes, it's Miss Webb, Sir Henry Hartley's secretary, speaking ... Oh, are you? ... No, Inspector, I'm sorry, he's not expected back from Hamburg till the week-end ... Yes, at least I suppose so ... Very well, I'll enter you in his book for 11 o'clock on Monday morning – subject of course to him not being detained elsewhere ... No, I can't make it any earlier, he doesn't like being disturbed while he's looking through his mail ... Thank you, Inspector Robertson – oh, so sorry, I'm altering it now ... Goodbye, Inspector Richardson.'

Mr Livesey, Third Officer and next on the list for interviewing, lived along the Southport line and happened to be in that afternoon when Richardson called to see him.

Mr Livesey expressed complete willingness to help but didn't think he could say much to amplify what he'd told the Pilotage Committee. Being new to the Company and this having been his first – and also last – voyage in the *Samarai*, he hardly knew the pilot. Yes, he'd seen him take her to the Bar Lightship on the outward voyage and had thought him competent: he'd therefore been surprised – perhaps he ought to have said shocked – by his handling of the ship immediately prior to the accident ... Yes, he knew Donovan better and considered him an excellent quartermaster – and a reliable man at the wheel too in his own limited experience of him. No, from his memory of events at the time of the grounding he didn't think Donovan could have averted it. In fact Donovan's contribution to the accident had seemed to him so minimal that the reprimand he'd been given struck him as being a bit hard ... Yes, from his personal point of view it had been a real disaster too. For he was still waiting for a job – companies weren't needing junior deck officers nowadays though had he been an engineer officer the situation would be different ... He was sorry he couldn't assist the police more; he didn't of course know what they suspected but for what it was worth his own opinion had been, and still was, that the whole thing had been due to the pilot being guilty of an error of judgment which on account of the limits imposed by the narrow width of the channel he couldn't rectify in time.

Richardson thanked him and drove away to the Princes Park area of Liverpool to interview the First Officer, Mr Burton. His address turned out to be a superior lodging house of the kind which likes to call itself a private hotel. Its door was opened by an elderly well-spoken woman who said Mr Burton had now left, having flown to Australia a week ago. From what he'd told her she understood the cable which arrived for him at the hotel a few days previously contained the offer of command of a ship engaged in the Australian coastal trade and owned by relatives of his who lived in Sydney. Yes, Mr Burton had once told her he was an Australian by birth, and with the unexpected loss of his ship which she thought had some name like *Samaritan* he told her he welcomed the offer and would be more than pleased to return to his native land.

3

(October 21)

There are fifty or more detached houses along Broadhurst Drive in the desirable Aigburth area of Liverpool, and when advertised for sale they are usually called residences. Nearly all have a name and no number, and just after four o'clock Richardson pulled up beside the open gateway of the villa he was looking for. He had phoned the pilotage office earlier in the day and learned from the Shoremaster that Gosling, having been ordered to join an outward-bound ship in the north end docks at half past six, was very likely to be at home during the afternoon.

For a short while Richardson sat on in his car, studying 'Marina's' red-tiled roof and stuccoed walls with nicely painted window frames. The shrubs in the small front garden were trim and tidy too. A broad strip of tarmac ran across it from gateway to garage; the narrower path of concrete veering off from it and leading to the front door had been chased to resemble crazy-paving. That chimney must have smoked, Richardson thought – one of the low pots on the central stack had been replaced by a galvanized pipe with a revolving cowl.

After locking his car he walked through the gateway. The garage doors were open and a dark green Ford saloon stood within. In passing he made a subconscious note of its registration number, and he pressed the bell-button beside the white-enamelled front door. Without undue delay and in answer to its chiming ring a full-figured woman with clear complexion and a mass of dark hair appeared in the doorway and looked at him with inquiring blue eyes.

Dismissing as irrelevant the thought that she was probably very good in bed, he said, 'I'm a police officer investigating the *Samarai* and I believe Mr Gosling can help me. Is he in?'

'Yes, he's in. But this isn't a very convenient time for him, he's going out soon to a ship.'

'Please say I won't detain him long.'

It was not imagination which told him she had become tense, and after a brief pause for thought she said, 'I'll let him know you're here.' She left him and went upstairs.

He heard the two of them talking, and when she came down she asked him to wait in the lounge and said her husband would be with him shortly. Leading the way, she switched on the big electric fire and departed.

Richardson, interested as always in the way of life of other people, began studying everything around him ... I don't like these modern carpets, he thought. And I don't like the picture of Swiss mountains or the Canadian Rockies in the gilt frame ... The TV set's quite nice on those legs but the piano's much too big for the size of the room, I suppose all that stuff on top of it must be music ... They don't go in for books here. No flowers either ... He now moved towards the fireplace. I wouldn't mind both of these, he thought, examining the pair of china horses, each with jockey up, which stood one on either side of the presentation clock occupying the middle of the mantelshelf ... My God, it's cold in here, the imitation logs are glowing fine but she was too upset to switch the bars on ... He looked out of the window – nothing to be seen except the privet hedge shielding 'Marina' from its next-door neighbour.

Gosling entered in dressing-gown and bedroom slippers. 'Sorry to have kept you waiting. My wife's told you I'm going out shortly on an all-night job and as you see I've got to get ready and have a meal first.'

'Sorry to have come at the wrong moment.'

'Don't worry about that. Make it as short as you can and I'll do my best to help you.' He was neither hostile nor friendly and he had forgotten to brush his hair.

'Won't you sit down? What do you want to know?'

'First let me tell you you're not compelled to answer my questions.'

Gosling laughed. 'That sounds a bit ominous. Go right ahead, I've nothing to conceal.'

'Are you contemplating early retirement from the pilotage service?'

The question surprised Gosling. 'As a matter of fact I am. But I haven't yet decided when.'

'Is that why you recently bought a property in the Channel Islands?'

'What the hell's that got to do with the *Samarai*?'

'I've nothing at all to ask you about the ship itself.'

'Oh, haven't you? ... Yes, we did get a smallish house, not a property as you call it, in Jersey. But I'd no intention of leaving the service, I hadn't blotted my copybook then.'

'How recently was the purchase made?'

'Completion date was about five months ago. But the preliminary negotiations started much earlier. And there was the survey too.'

'To change the subject I understand you're a betting man and have had some good successes. I'd like to hear something about them.'

Again Gosling seemed surprised. 'Well, I may as well admit I've always been a bit of a punter, on the whole a lucky one. Of course I've had my losses too.'

'I'd rather hear about your recent wins. The bigger ones.'

'I picked up quite a packet on an outsider named Golden Boy at Sandown the summer before last and I had another big win on Mazurka on the last race of the second day at Ripon a few weeks later.' On his own subject Gosling spoke without restraint. 'The bookies were caught napping there, I got 5 to 1. I don't know about you but I never bet on the classic races, the odds aren't good enough.'

Richardson was entering the names in his book. 'Wish I was equally clever ... And now please give me the name of your bookmaker.'

Gosling's sallow cheeks flushed. 'Aren't you now going too far?' he objected hotly.

'I can find out if you wish. I was just hoping you'd save me the trouble.'

After consideration or perhaps because he was pressed for time Gosling swallowed his indignation and said, 'I've several, not all on Merseyside. There's Bert Ramsden of Leeds for one and Moorhouse of Morecambe for another. And Dave Davies here in Liverpool.'

Richardson entered the names and put his book away. 'That's all, Mr Gosling. Thanks for being so co-operative.'

Gosling laughed again. 'You haven't given me much chance of being otherwise.'

'Sorry, that's my job,' Richardson said with a smile. 'I make my living asking questions.'

CHAPTER X

(October 24)

1

Miss Beatrice Webb rose gracefully from her desk and greeted Richardson with the accomplished smile reserved exclusively for the Company's visitors from outside. 'Inspector Richardson of course? ... Sir Henry will be glad to see you at once.'

Moving with elegance she threw open the mahogany door which those in the office who disliked her said she guarded more zealously than her virtue, and in stepping past he wondered if she knew all Sir Henry's secrets or only some of them.

In the centre of the large well-proportioned room stood what the office-furnishing trade term a chief executive's desk – in this case a king-sized piece with a flat top and made throughout from some exotic wood. Behind it sat enthroned Sir Henry.

Richardson moved towards him across the thick pile of the silver-grey carpet. His trained eye had already noted windows curtained with dull crimson silk, panelled walls painted just-off white, two dreary portraits in heavily gilded frame of a man with a beard and a man without – the defunct Shanklin Brothers, had he known – and, much more alive, a vivid modern oil-painting of a New Guinea landscape with savage peaks and lush tropical forest.

'Good morning, Inspector. Please sit down.' Sir Henry indicated the leather-covered chair close beside his desk, and Richardson, all too conscious of the shabby state of his everyday and only mackintosh, dropped into it gingerly and found it even softer than it looked. By now the mental photograph he had secured of the owner of all this opulence showed a well-groomed and well-clothed but otherwise quite ordinary man, no doubt handsome once but now becoming bald and stoutish. His mouth was strong and there were bags under tired eyes.

'Care to smoke?' A silver cigarette-box was pushed forward. 'Or do you prefer a New Guinea cheroot?' The culture in Sir Henry's voice was as natural as though inbred.

'No thanks, I'll stick to cigarettes. I've come for your help, Sir Henry. I'm investigating certain aspects of the loss of your ship and hoping you can clear up some points we'd like to know more about.' To any experienced police officer all men are equal when under interrogation, and Richardson spoke accordingly.

Wreathed in smoke from the cheroot he had just lit, Sir Henry replied, 'I know there have been some strange rumours about my ship but the fact remains she was the victim of an accident – an accident which should never have occurred, let me add.'

'We pay no attention to rumours, Sir Henry. We work on facts.'

'Quite.' Sir Henry glanced for some seconds at the smoke ring ascending steadily to the ceiling. 'What do you want to know from me?'

'More than we know already about the affairs of your ex-pilot Mr Gosling.'

'I presume you mean his private affairs. Why do you expect me to know about them?'

'I'll explain. I understand before you engaged him you were advised of his reputation as a betting man?

That he was in fact a gambler?'

'Yes, Armstrong the head of the pilotage put me wise to that. But he also assured me he was an exceptionally good pilot. Otherwise I shouldn't have engaged him – the fact that he happens to have married my niece carried no weight at all with me.'

'I understand that, Sir Henry. During the time of his employment with you had you any knowledge of the extent of his betting wins and losses? For instance that his winnings on certain races presumably enabled him to buy a house in the Channel Islands?'

Sir Henry looked surprised. 'Who told you that?'

'He told me himself about the house, also about some of his bigger wins. I assumed the two went together.'

'Your assumption is wrong, Inspector,' Sir Henry said tartly. '*I* bought the house.'

'*You*, Sir Henry?' It was Richardson's turn to show surprise. 'May I ask why?'

'To give to my niece of course. It's her house, not her husband's.'

'When did you buy it and give it to her?'

'My solicitors can tell you the exact date. The purchase was handled entirely by them.'

'I don't need the exact date. Was it this year? Or last?'

'Some time in the spring of this year.'

'So far as you know was her husband contemplating retirement from the pilotage service at the time of the purchase?'

'I'm not sufficiently in his confidence to be able to answer that.' When irritated Sir Henry's voice became sardonic.

'I'd like to return to a previous question. I asked if you had any knowledge of the extent of his betting wins and losses during the period of his employment with you. Are you aware of any?'

'Not of his wins. But I happen to know something of his losses.' Sir Henry's voice now became dry.

'How substantial were they?'

'That depends on what you mean by substantial. They were considerably more so to him than to me. The two of which I know amounted in total to well over a thousand pounds.'

'How was he able to meet them?'

'He wasn't able to meet them. I paid them myself, Inspector.'

'May I ask why you did that?'

'I had my reasons of course. My niece was naturally very worried, I suppose that was the strongest reason. And I gather the publicity involved in the event of his bookmaker trying to hammer him might have caused him to resign from the pilotage service, and I certainly didn't wish to lose a pilot who in all other ways had proved exemplary and who was handling ships of mine worth several millions.'

'Thank you, Sir Henry. I've nothing more to ask you.'

Sir Henry held up his hand. 'One moment. Since you've succeeded in uncovering this skeleton in our family cupboard I'm going to amplify what I've already told you. The reason I bought the house in Jersey for my niece was to give her a much-needed sense of security. And I don't mind telling you too that the second time her husband came to me about his betting losses I said I'd pay them this once more. But never again, I told him categorically, whatever the circumstances.'

'I understand. Thank you for all your help and for being so frank.'

Sir Henry's smile was cordial, and on this amiable note the interview ended.

*   *   *

In passing through Miss Webb's room on his way out Richardson brushed shoulders with a man who was no stranger and who was obviously waiting there to go inside, and though each looked hard at the other neither spoke. Why the hell's *he* here, Richardson wondered, and Gosling wondered the same thing.

Sir Henry was wondering too, for Miss Webb had been unable to enlighten him.

'He wouldn't say,' she explained. 'He phoned nearly a week ago for an appointment and when I told him you were on the continent he said he'd got to see you the first possible moment after you returned.'

'He didn't say why?'

'No, only that it was an urgent family matter. So I told him to come today at 11.30 and he wanted to come earlier but I wouldn't let him – you won't have visitors before 11 and I'd just already booked Inspector Richardson for then.'

Sir Henry nodded wearily. 'As he's here I'll see him. Please send him in.'

2

During the afternoon of that same day Chief Inspector Young and Richardson chanced to meet on the stone stairway of the Divisional office. 'Making headway?' Young asked.

'Some, sir. But not as much as I'd hoped. Enough to know it's going to be a difficult one to crack.'

'Seen them all yet?'

'All except the ship's captain. I don't expect he'll have much to tell me so I'm leaving him till the last.'

Young nodded. 'Come and talk to me about it when you've seen him.'

'Very good, sir. I'd intended to go there this afternoon but I started the shivers before lunch and now I've a headache too. It could be 'flu starting.'

Young nodded again. 'I hear there's a lot of it about. You'd better come to my room now and tell me how far you've got, and then clear off home.'

Following Young into his room Richardson refused the cigarette offered, sat as close to the fire as he could, and said, 'I've been so well briefed these last few days that though my previous knowledge of ships and pilotage was nil I think I know enough now to say there's something fishy in all this. But as Armstrong the pilotage superintendent said to me no one can ever prove from what happened on the bridge that the pilot wrecked the ship on purpose. Donovan the quartermaster is quite sure he did, and so of course is Williams from what he let fly at the Pilotage Committee's inquiry. Beecher the company's marine superintendent probably thinks so too though he's not admitting it in so many words. If there's a conspiracy somewhere – and I think myself there is – it lies in the tight little family triangle of the pilot and his wife and Sir Henry.

'So far the only thing I've been able to get my teeth into is Gosling the pilot's betting losses. I've now collected a list of them from the bookies he named, his winnings too, and the list's in my room though you won't need to see it. What's much more material is that his losses during the past couple of years have been substantial, so substantial that on two occasions – the last one being only some months ago – Sir Henry had to pay them. I say "had to" because he told me if he hadn't Gosling might have been hammered and in that event compelled to leave the service, and in consequence Sir Henry would have lost him as a pilot. In other words Sir Henry was prepared to fork out between a thousand

and fifteen hundred to keep him, and there must be some significance in that.

'And now we come to the house in Jersey. When talking to Gosling I'd jumped to the conclusion he'd bought it himself and never thought of questioning him further about it. But he hadn't. Sir Henry volunteered he'd bought it himself and given it to his niece as a present. Towards the end of our talk he opened up and admitted the real reason he'd bought it for her was to give her security, and he inferred he thought precious little of her husband except as a pilot. Mind you Sir Henry's presumably still a rich man and getting on in years, and I've learned elsewhere Mrs Gosling's his only niece and they've been on close and affectionate terms for years. So you can't fault him for giving her a costly present if he wants to.

'But my suspicious mind tells me it could all add up to a kind of quid pro quo – I'll pay your betting losses and buy your wife a nice house and see you right afterwards if you'll wreck my ship. But it's another thing to prove it. Of course it's true his Company hasn't been doing so well of recent years and I've learned from your prim friend in the insurance company it's commonly held it has no future with things and politics as they now are in New Guinea. Even so I'd guess from his surroundings and the way he lives he's even now got plenty of spending money. All the same I'd like to see his bank account though I know I can't – not yet. So where do we go from there?'

'Nowhere at the moment. Be patient, Bob, and put the file aside and forget about it for the time being. And send back the *Samarai* papers to the insurance company, you can always borrow them again if you need them. This is the kind of case in which big financial issues are involved, and sooner or later in my experience money always talks. I'm no betting man like your pilot but I'd lay short odds you'll get a break before very long. And now get off home and take some aspirins and go to bed. You're looking rotten.'

CHAPTER XI

(October 25)

Wirral, that small peninsula in Cheshire bounded on
three sides by the Mersey and the Dee, has long been
a dormitory of Liverpool, and even today there is room
– though not very much – for a few more beds. Of its
numerous villages and townships Burton is still the
pleasantest, Willaston and Parkgate coming second or
third according to taste. This relatively undeveloped
area of Wirral contains some large and expensive houses
and estates, of which one, the Lydiate, fortuitously enters
this story. Invisible from most directions, the house
itself stands half a mile from Willaston off the right
hand side of the road from Birkenhead; a Liverpool
shipowner built it and lived in it for more than a genera-
tion. Then it became the property of a wealthy cotton-
broker who helped to make ends meet by becoming a
leading banker as well. The cotton-broker having died,
it was now standing empty, deserted, and for sale.

From the Birkenhead road and through the Lydiate's
surrounding farmland runs a dog-legged lane, used as a
short cut by the limited number of travellers who prefer
this unfrequented route to any other and continue by
Damhead Lane, another narrow road, to the Chester
highway or perhaps across it to Deeside townships such
as Neston. Hardly a quarter of a mile in length, this
short cut, which is nameless, has a right-angle bend in
its middle, and here, close to the bend and at about half
past seven on a damp and misty evening in late October,
a commercial traveller in ladies' underwear driving
home after a long and tiring day in industrial Lanca-

shire saw a motorcar which had crashed through the wooden fence into the field beyond.

He stopped, got out, and tapped on one of the car's windows. Receiving no reply, he opened the door and concluded the man slumped over the steering-wheel with his hatless head against the windscreen was either dead or very ill. Realizing there was nothing he could usefully do himself he returned to his car and drove a couple of miles out of his way to Neston police station, where at 7.46 p.m. – according to the station book – he told the constable in the office what he had seen.

'Your name and address, sir, if you please ... Exact location of the car?'

'In the short cut by the Lydiate.'

'At what time did you see it?'

'I didn't look at my watch. About ten minutes ago, say.'

'Did you recognize the driver?'

'No. A man, that's all.'

'Was he alone in the car?'

'So far as I could see, yes.'

'Thanks for informing us and we'll attend to it.'

The motorist went and the constable slipped round to the sergeant's quarters next door. The sergeant and his wife had just started supper.

'You say the informant believes the driver is dead?'

'Yes, sarge.'

'Could he identify him?'

'He said not.'

'Ring Clatterbridge Hospital for an ambulance and say I'll be there to meet it. Is the car on or off the road?'

'Off, he said. Through the fence and into the field.'

'Ring Macandrew's Garage as well and tell him to send along his towing vehicle.'

*   *   *

The sergeant in his black Morris was the first to arrive. He instantly identified the car and its occupant, and his knowledge of first aid confirmed that he was dead. He next examined the road ... Not a skid mark anywhere, it couldn't have been a dog or a fox he was avoiding. And he couldn't have been doing more than twenty after coming round the bend ... A careful policeman, he now flashed his torch round the car inside and out to satisfy himself things were as they appeared to be and that there was no evidence of violence. He noted the man's position, his body across the wheel with his right foot on the brake pedal. He noted that the inside driving-mirror fixed above the centre of the windscreen was smashed. He also noted that one headlamp and both sidelights had been broken by the fence whereas all other lights were working. He put his hand inside the car and touched the dead man's ungloved hand. Strange, he thought, it's colder than I was expecting, why should that be? ... Maybe he'd sat here quite a while before being seen and reported, it's not everyone who'll stop these days ... He glanced at the dashboard clock; it was still working and gave no clue.

Then what was the explanation? ... That's it, he must have automatically pulled to the left and tried to brake when he fainted or felt a heart attack coming on ... The grass round the car's trampled a bit, likely that was done by the chap who found him – he said at the station he'd opened the door and looked at him ... Well, it all seems straightforward enough to me and I've seen a few in my time ... No measurements needed and I wouldn't get any thanks for sending for the photographers...

The rain was now beginning and he went back to his car and put on his cape. Next he waved on a passing motorist who showed signs of stopping, and he was entering up his notes when the ambulance from Clatter-bridge arrived.

Its driver knew the sergeant. 'How many for us to-day?' he asked.

'Only one and he hasn't been certified. Dead when I got here.'

In the police world no one is properly dead till certified dead by a doctor. Moreover the sergeant was well aware that all ambulance drivers dislike uncertified bodies, because as well as having to wait at the accident unit while the death certificate is being prepared, they are sometimes landed with the extra job of searching the body and laying it out themselves when ultimately offloaded at the mortuary.

The ambulance driver shook his head. 'Posh car. Who's the bloke?'

'Sir Henry Hartley.'

'Him, eh? ... Looks dead all right to me.'

'Remember, will you, to ask the casualty officer if he can state approximate time of death. He felt on the cold side to me when I touched him a quarter of an hour ago.'

'O.K., sarge. Do we go ahead now or wait till you've had him photoed?'

'No photograph for this one. Seems like natural causes to me and anyhow there'll be the P.M.'

'O.K.,' the ambulance driver said, and called to his mate, 'Bring the stretcher, Ted. One more for the slab ... Coming with us, sarge?'

'No, not today. I've his car to see to.'

They were lifting Sir Henry from his driving seat when the lights of the towing vehicle appeared and the sergeant walked away to meet it. When he looked back the ambulance had gone.

Mr Macandrew was driving the towing vehicle and

he lived up to his reputation as a man of silence. Though recognizing the car and though Sir Henry was one of his customers – and a better payer than most – he spoke only three words. 'Where to, Sergeant?'

'Put it on the police station park and tell the duty-constable to make sure all its doors are properly locked. It'll be staying there till after the P.M.' The sergeant suddenly wondered if after all he should have sent for the police photographers.

Mr Macandrew came of farming stock and spoke again. 'How about yon broken fence?'

'It can wait till morning. I've looked and there aren't no animals in the field.'

When the sergeant returned to his house at half-past nine his wife opened the oven door and glanced at his half-eaten chop. 'There's another in the larder, dear, and I'd better cook it for you. But there's no more veg.'

He inspected the shrivelled remains. 'Don't bother, this one'll do.'

In telling her what had happened he said he'd been to the Old Hall to break the news to Lady Hartley.

'Poor thing. How did she take it?'

'A sight better than you if it'd been me. You'd think she didn't care.'

Here the sergeant was being unjust. Lady Hartley had learned to control her feelings, and the news neither shocked nor surprised her. But she did care. Indeed she was very sorry, her sorrow being largely for herself because of the change she knew her husband's death was likely to bring to her personal affluence and easy way of life.

CHAPTER XII

1

(October 26)

Under the caption 'SUDDEN DEATH OF PROMINENT CITY SHIPOWNER' Sir Henry filled the whole of a centre-page column in Wednesday's *Daily Post*. The head-and-shoulders portrait which accompanied it bore small resemblance to the heavy and ageing personage whom friends and acquaintances knew; it had been lifted and enlarged from a photograph taken nine or ten years earlier outside Buckingham Palace on the day of the award of his K.B.E., and showed a smiling middle-aged man in the best of health with hair erupting from under the sides of his top-hat. The column gave an excellent potted account of the passage through life of a Liverpool boy who by grit and determination had progressed to become a figure of international importance in the shipping world. No mention was made of the *Samarai*, and the column ended with a paragraph to the effect that the deceased, having left his office at the usual time, had suffered a sudden and fatal illness on the roadside while driving to his residence at Ness near Burton. A passing motorist, Mr A. M. Brown, noticed him in a state of collapse inside his motorcar and had stopped in the hope of rendering assistance. An ambulance was summoned but on arrival at Clatterbridge Hospital Sir Henry was found to be dead. Funeral arrangements would be notified later after a post-mortem had been held.

* * *

By eight o'clock that morning the white and blue houseflag on the staff below the big copper dome on the roof of the Dockboard building could be seen flying at half-mast. It was hardly noticed by the majority of Merseysiders hurrying to their shops and offices from the Corporation bus terminal at the Pier Head or from the ferry-steamers scuttling to and fro across the Mersey; the few who saw it and who had not read their papers merely wondered, if they wondered at all, which member or forgotten ex-member of the Board was dead. But the initiated – and these included many of Liverpool's shipping and insurance and bigger business world – knew, some with envy and some with resentment, that the Dockboard was still Liverpool's most honoured institution and were thus aware that the Dockboard flag at half-mast signified a message of exclusiveness and distinction now being transmitted to heaven and the grave.

Chief Inspector Young saw the photograph and caption while eating his bacon and egg, and on arriving at the Divisional office rang down at once to inquire if any sick report had come in from Richardson.

'No, sir. Matter of fact it's Richardson speaking.'

'Didn't I send you home on Monday as you were starting 'flu?'

'It wasn't 'flu, sir. I took the aspirins as you said and stayed in bed all day yesterday, and this morning I woke feeling fine. So here I am. Anything you want, sir?'

'Yes. Read your *Daily Post* this morning?'

'No sir, we don't take it, we have the *Telegraph*. I can't afford both.'

'You'd better afford it this morning.' Richardson heard Young's chuckle as he rang off.

He sent out for a copy, saw the caption, and told himself what his eyes saw couldn't possibly be true. As he read on, his subconscious mind began grappling with the probable consequences of this inescapable new fact. He reached the end of the column and thought hard for a few seconds. Then he picked up his telephone and spoke first to Neston police station, getting an immediate answer to the few simple questions he asked. Next he telephoned to a friend in Chester, an inspector in Cheshire CID named Bird.

'Morning, Dicky. Bob Richardson here and needing your help.'

'What sort of help?'

'According to my morning paper Sir Henry Hartley died in his car in your parish yesterday evening. Between you and me I've got a file on him and it's still open.'

'Hartley? The man who owned the *Samarai*?'

'That's the chap. Apparently there's to be a P.M. and I'd like to hear quickly if anything out of the ordinary is found.'

'Suspecting something?'

'Could be. Though it's just as likely to be straight Natural Causes, he wasn't looking so well when I visited him at the beginning of this week.'

'Right, Bob. I'll have a word with the Coroner's officer now and tell him to let me know at once if anything sinister's found. Anything else?'

'Not at the moment. Thanks a lot and good-bye for now.'

After two or three more brief but informative telephone calls Richardson sent for a map of Wirral, studied it for five minutes, and finally went upstairs to Chief Inspector Young.

Young, his desk-top uncluttered as usual, was smoking his pipe. 'Any theory?' he asked.

'No, sir. But quite a discrepancy.' Richardson spread

113

out the map. 'According to his secretary he left his office at his usual time of soon after five, and when I asked why he was driving himself she said he did sometimes because he preferred it to being driven. How often was "sometimes", I asked her, and she said perhaps twice or three times a month. Neston police station say he was reported to them at 7.46 p.m., the informant having said he'd found him about ten minutes earlier. That means he took two hours or more to cover the twelve miles between his office and the spot where he was found. Which is here.' Richardson pointed to the spot he had ringed on the map.

'Continue.'

'The Tunnel police say there were no breakdowns or serious delays in any of the lanes to Birkenhead yesterday afternoon or evening and that traffic flowed normally all the time except during the normal rush-hour congestion. So I've allowed ten minutes for that. The Neston sergeant says the minor road where he and his car were found – it's a short by-pass really, a short cut between two bigger roads – is never busy but never entirely traffic-free except by night. So I'm allowing half an hour from the time he collapsed till the time he was seen by the chap who stopped. That may of course be too generous but it doesn't matter much. And now I come to the point. Where was he and what was he doing during the hour and a quarter or hour and a half not accounted for?'

'What kind of car was he driving?'

'His own. A Mercedes. They don't break down, I'd thought of that.'

'Have you also thought he may have a bird somewhere on his way home and felt the urge to call in and see her? Tycoons often have and do, you know. That would account for him driving himself and dispensing with his chauffeur several times a month.'

'Are you really serious, sir? A man of his age?'

'Age has nothing to do with it and when you're a bit older yourself you'll know that as well as I do.' Young's eyes twinkled. 'I'm not claiming my theory's correct but at least it's possible and I mention it now in case you're wanting a new line of inquiry to work on.'

It was Young's little way of telling Richardson he was well pleased with the way things were going.

Later that morning Captain Armstrong rang up Richardson. 'I suppose you know Sir Henry Hartley died yesterday?' he said, quiet-voiced as always.

'Yes, we do know that.'

'His death has reminded me of a small incident which slipped my memory when you called the other day. It's got nothing to do with Sir Henry however, it's only about Williams.'

'Yes? Would you like me to come over?' Richardson wondered if this was going to be his lucky day.

'Don't bother because it's no more than this. A week or ten days ago Williams turned up for lunch on the *Landfall* and happened to come and sit beside me. Though very silent at first he suddenly became talkative and asked me if Gosling was working that afternoon. I told him I'd no idea and if he really wanted to know he'd better ask the Shoremaster. Knowing the bad blood existing between Williams and Gosling I was slightly surprised, and next day out of curiosity I asked the Shoremaster if Williams had questioned him about Gosling. Yes he had, the Shoremaster said, and added how surprised he was too. I'm afraid that's all, but it does appear as if for some reason Williams must have been anxious to get in touch with Gosling.'

'Thanks. This could be quite useful – provided Sir

Henry's death hasn't put paid to the whole inquiry.'

'I never thought of that. How sorry would you be if it had?'

Richardson laughed. 'That's a hundred dollar question! ... I'd be sorry. I suppose ... Yes, in fact damned sorry.'

2

(October 28)

The Coroner's officer was a middle-aged police constable liked by all because of his humanity in dealing with the distressed and because he remained unruffled by the macabre nature of his job – which included assisting the pathologist at post-mortems. When Sir Henry's was over he went to the nearest public telephone and rang up Detective-Inspector Bird.

'Sir, the pathologist's in no doubt cause of death was coronary artery disease and in the casualty officer's opinion death occurred an hour and a half to two hours before seeing the body at the accident unit. Over the left temple bone there was a small laceration only about an inch long but quite deep. Must have bled a lot, and what surprised us was that some of the blood – not all of it, sir – had been washed or wiped away. What surprised us as much was the fragment of glass from the car's broken driving-mirror found in the laceration, there's no obvious explanation for that unless someone had placed it there ... No, sir, dead bodies bleed for quite a time after death and it's virtually impossible to say whether the injury occurred before death or after.'

'When's the adjourned inquest?'*

* A very brief preliminary inquest had already been held for the purpose of formal identification only.

'The Coroner won't have fixed it yet. Some day next week, I expect.'

'Let me know time and place as soon as he does. I'll want to have a word with him beforehand.'

(*November 2*)

Originally designed and built to serve the nation as a workhouse, the Clatterbridge of today is a vast and ever-growing hospital, and there in one of its older blocks the adjourned inquest took place at 11 o'clock in the forenoon in a concert hall temporarily rearranged to form a court-room.

The proceedings did not last long and before they began the Coroner noted the presence of Detective-Inspector Bird and a man with him he did not recognize but rightly suspected to be another police officer. Lady Hartley was also present, becomingly dressed in black and accompanied by an elderly and equally well-dressed woman whom he guessed was her mother.

The questions and answers which interested Richardson most were:

CORONER: You have said this man had coronary artery disease which in your opinion was the cause of death?

PATHOLOGIST: Yes.

CORONER: You have also told us there was a small laceration over the left temple bone. In your opinion was this in any way responsible for precipitating the fatal attack?

PATHOLOGIST: It is not impossible. I would not go further than that.

CORONER: Is there any evidence to show how or when the laceration was caused?

PATHOLOGIST: No, none whatsoever.

Since either by accident or design the Coroner did not labour this point neither of the two reporters present thought it worth writing down. But their pens got very busy when to the surprise of the few present but not to Bird or Richardson the Coroner announced quietly and quickly that on grounds which could not be disclosed he was adjourning the inquest for a week to enable certain inquiries to be completed. Then, as though to smother the sensation his words had caused, he went on as quietly to express his own sympathy and that of the court with Lady Hartley on the loss she had sustained, and that ended the proceedings.

Bird and Richardson left the court-room together, and Bird said to Richardson, 'Let's go now to Neston police station to speak to the sergeant about Hartley's car. It's still on his park and I want to ring Chester and arrange for its interior to be given the works and for its front seats and carpets to go this afternoon to the lab at Preston. And then we'll have a pint somewhere.'

'That suits me. And after that with your permission I'd like to call and have a few words with Lady Hartley.'

From Neston police station they drove to Willaston, where over beer and sandwiches in the Nags Head they talked shop. They had known each other for a number of years, and though of different types had become good friends. Unlike Richardson – an extrovert even when questioning suspects – Bird was withdrawn and so scholarly in appearance that those who did not know his occupation could hardly have guessed it. His high reputation as a thoughtful and thorough worker was based on an early achievement when as a detective-constable he spent a year unravelling a complicated case of fraud. It ended with the conviction of four men and a woman, and after sentencing them the assize judge complimented him and said that in his experience few young police officers could have shown greater patience, acumen, and skill. Bird's chief constable, in those days an ex-army officer but not much worse for that, had noted the judge's remarks, and thereafter Bird's promotions had been steady and not unduly deferred.

They were driving after lunch from Willaston to Ness Old Hall, and Bird said, 'One of us is quite enough for her today. What you're asking her is no direct concern of mine so I'll sit in the car and wait.'

From the curve in its long drive they saw the mellow sandstone house with its mullioned windows and surrounding lawns surrounded in turn by spinneys and specimen trees, and as Bird pulled up in the forecourt Richardson said, 'Whatever worries he had at the office he can't have had many in a place like this.'

A bell-pull of wrought iron hung beside the heavy oak door, and Richardson told the manservant who answered his ring who he was and said if Lady Hartley would excuse him for coming on such a day he'd like to speak to her for a few minutes.

'I'll inquire of her ladyship, sir.'

Richardson was admiring the view across the lawns through the windows of the beautifully furnished room into which he had been shown when Lady Hartley entered. No longer dressed in black, she looked pale and apprehensive and said at once, 'Oh, haven't I just seen you at the inquest?'

'You have. It's my case in a way and I came over from Liverpool for it. I do hope you'll forgive me for coming to see you on a day like this – '

'Please don't apologize. I'm quite glad you're here because what happened this morning came as a great shock to us and I'm hoping you can explain the reason for the adjournment.'

'I can't yet, I'm afraid. We're still only probing and thinking things mayn't be quite what they appear to be. We're satisfied Sir Henry died from a heart attack but we think something could have occurred beforehand to bring it on. I'm sorry I can't say more than that.'

'My mother and I guessed it must be something like that. What have you come to ask me about?'

'About a few things which still perplex us. For instance I understand Sir Henry had a chauffeur?'

'Yes, we have.'

'Then why should he be driving himself on the day of his death?'

'You may well ask. I've always been opposed to it and often told him he had far too much on his mind to drive really well. To answer your question he drove because he so enjoyed driving, and he was always looking for an excuse to drive more.'

'What do you mean by "excuse"?'

'The Tuesday he died happened to be Frank's weekly day off – Frank's our chauffeur and when not chauffeuring he's our manservant and valet – and my husband was very considerate about not disturbing the free days of anyone we employ.'

'So about once a week Sir Henry drove himself?'

'No, not as often as that. When it happened to be Frank's day off and my husband had a busy day ahead the office always sent a car for him.'

'Presumably the office didn't do so that Tuesday because he wasn't expecting a busy day?'

'I suppose he'd have said that. As I've told you he was always looking for excuses.'

'At what time did he normally arrive home from the office, whether driving himself or being driven?'

'The times of course varied. Sometimes quite early in the afternoon, sometimes just in time for dinner. But his normal time would be about six.'

'I take it you were worried about his apparent lateness on the evening he died?'

'Of course I was. So much so that I telephoned the office to find out if he'd been detained.'

'What did they tell you?'

'Miss Webb his secretary was still there and said he'd left about five and she seemed as concerned as I was. That made me more worried still and I felt sure he must have had an accident.'

'I well understand how you felt. Would it surprise you to know from the time he left his office till he reached the place of the accident and after taking all the probable time-lags into account, there's still an hour and a half unaccounted for?'

'It surprises me very much.'

'Do you know of anything to explain this missing hour and a half?'

'I'm very sorry I don't.'

'Excuse me for asking you this, Lady Hartley. Do you know of any man or woman friend Sir Henry might have visited on his way home?'

She paused for a moment as though trying to find the right words with which to express herself. 'He wasn't ever the kind of man to have a woman friend of the sort I suppose you mean. As for a man friend I can't think of anyone between the office and where he was found, not of the kind you just drop in on at least. And I'm certain he'd have told me or asked Miss Webb to let me know if he'd been intending to call somewhere – he was considerate about that too.' She smiled for the first time. 'He had to be – we've a good cook and we don't want to lose her.'

'Did he say anything to you during breakfast on Tuesday morning or before leaving for the office to indicate he wasn't returning home direct that evening?'

'He didn't. And if he had I'd remember because we never talked much at breakfast. He liked reading his paper undisturbed.'

'Had he spoken to you recently about any office worries he may have had? Apart from the *Samarai*?'

'No, we hardly ever talked about business affairs, I'm afraid he thought I couldn't understand them.'

'A final question. Do you know of any local enemies he had?'

'I don't know of one. Nobody's been dismissed from here for years. Though of course he travelled a lot abroad and overseas, and a man in his position is bound to make some. But I can't give you any names.'

'Thank you for all your help. I'm sure some of the things you've told me will prove useful.'

'She's a sensible woman all right and she's trying to help,' Richardson told Bird as he returned to the car. 'But she knows nothing to account for that missing hour and a half.'

'Then shall we go to Rock Ferry and talk to Williams? You said you haven't questioned him yet, and isn't it possible he's among the very few who do know something?'

'Possible, yes. But likely, no ... Anyhow let's go.'

3

A keen philatelist of many years' standing, Captain

Williams had taken advantage of his voyages to special-
ize in the stamps of Australia, New Guinea (formerly
New Britain), and the more juvenile Papua. His collection was of considerable value and he had of course seen
to it that the albums which contained it had been salved
from the safe in his cabin shortly after the *Samarai*'s
grounding.

He was seated at his table studying Queen Victoria's
profile on an 1854 New South Wales fourpenny when
the doorbell rang. Since Mrs Williams was shopping in
Birkenhead he got up to answer it and found two men
of respectable appearance standing on the doorstep.
'We're police officers wanting to speak to Captain
Williams,' the thinner one told him.

'You are speaking to him now.'

Though neither wore uniform he saw no reason to
disbelieve them, and as a supporter of the establishment
he could hardly refuse to ask them in. He therefore conducted them into the dining-room where, given any
encouragement, he would have been glad to show them
the treasures in the album open on the table.

But neither so much as glanced at it, and the thin one
spoke again and said, 'I am Detective-Inspector Bird of
Cheshire CID and this is my Liverpool colleague
Detective-Inspector Richardson and we're here on a
routine inquiry.'

Police protocol required Bird's presence because Rock
Ferry is in Cheshire, and that was why initially he acted
as spokesman. Hence Richardson was given time and
opportunity to look around, and being Richardson he
took it. Never before had he seen the walls of any room
so crowded with so many strange and junklike objects.
Photographs of ships and steamers ancient and modern
jostled for space with trophies such as a fan-like array
of primitive weapons, a hideous painted mask, and a

small roundish lump now shrunken and indeterminate but once the head of a Papuan tribesman. Close beside it, stretched out taut as though flying on its canvas-covered board, the faded pennant of some antipodean yacht club struck an incongruous but more civilized note.

'A routine inquiry about what?' Williams was asking, puzzled.

'In connection with the loss of the *Samarai*. Inspector Richardson here has been in charge of it for the past fortnight.'

'I did not know any such inquiry was taking place.' Williams sounded aggrieved, even affronted. 'If I had known I would have helped.'

'In what way, Captain?' It was Richardson who spoke.

'Never you mind. It is too late now. Justice has been done and I now wish to forget about the loss of my ship and everything connected with it.'

'I understand that, Captain. But how has justice been done?'

'The man responsible has been struck down.'

Bird spoke once more. 'If Hartley's the man you refer to, it's his death we're inquiring into.'

'He was killed by God. So why ask me?'

Richardson wondered if the man was batty. 'Inspector Bird's just told you this is a routine inquiry and we only want to know where you were between 6 and 8 on Tuesday evening of last week.'

'Oh, that is easily answered. I was sitting here in this room till about half past six and then I went to the Great Eastern hotel for a drink.'

'I know it,' Bird said in an aside to Richardson, and to Williams, 'Did Mrs Williams go with you?'

'Having been away she did not wish to.'

'I expect you met several of your friends at the hotel?'

124

'I do not call men I meet in any public house my friends.'

'Can you name anyone you met there that evening?'

'I have not troubled to learn their names. For many years until recently I have been away at sea for three months or more at a time, and my visits to the Great Eastern have been few and far between.'

'So you can't name a single person you met or spoke to at the Great Eastern during that evening?'

'I did not say that,' Williams retorted quite sharply. 'In ordering a drink I spoke to George the barman. I do not know his other name.'

'No one else?'

'No one I know by name as I have already told you.'

Bird had reached a dead end, and his face showed it. He glanced inquiringly at Richardson whose waiting question landed like a shell from an unexpected quarter. 'When did you last see Sir Henry Hartley?'

'I do not keep a diary and cannot truthfully give you the exact date.'

'The exact date doesn't matter. How long ago was it?'

'About a fortnight.'

'During the week before his death in fact?'

'Yes, that is it.'

'Where did you see him?'

'In his office.'

'Did you speak to him there?'

'Of course. I had gone specially for that purpose.'

'May I ask what you spoke to him about?'

'I was asking him to increase my pension.'

'Did he accede to your request?'

'He said he thought the rules of the Company's pension fund could be bent in my favour and promised to do his best to bring this about.'

'Have you seen or spoken to him since?'

'No.'

This ended the first questioning of Captain Williams by the police, and they departed together with mild expressions of regret for having disturbed him and of thanks for what they had been told. Moreover they seemed satisfied.

But Williams was far from satisfied. That they had not come to see him sooner irked him considerably – had they done so he would have been spared an immense amount of inconvenience and trouble. In all the circumstances he would not now lift a finger to help them. The past was past so far as he was concerned and the truest thing he had told them was that he now wished to forget the loss of his ship and everything connected with it. He turned the gas fire a little higher and went back to his stamps, and when Mrs Williams returned he did not think it worth mentioning that he had had two visitors.

George of the Great Eastern was no exception to the rule that barmen are co-operative with the police. Not yet raised to the status of a gin palace, the stone-faced pub in which he worked stands solid and four-square beside a grassy open space in close enough proximity to the Cheshire bank of the Mersey to justify its honoured and nostalgic name.

Yes, George told the two detectives, he knew Captain Williams though not what you might call well. The little old fellow with the black hair and Welsh way of speaking, wasn't he? He knew Mrs Williams better, she being the blondy one with the sticking-out tits who often came in with one or other of her boy-friends while the Captain was away at sea –

At this point he was checked by Bird.

Oh, not her? It was the Captain they were asking

about? And was he in between 6.30 and 8 on Tuesday of last week? Well, that wasn't an easy one to answer – most midweek evenings were alike between those times and busier than you'd think thanks to good money at Levers and Stork, Lairds too ... But now that he came to think of it the Captain did come in last Tuesday or Wednesday, he couldn't be quite certain which ... Yes, he remembered it now, the Captain had a double brandy and Mrs W a couple of ports and he put down a fiver and said he'd nothing less ... Likelier to be the Tuesday though not to swear to it, his business being attending to customers' glasses and not to their faces. Was there anything more he could tell them? No? Then would either of them care for one for the road? ... Not when on duty? A pity, but he understood and perhaps they'd look in and give him that pleasure next time they happened to be in the district ... Good afternoon, gentlemen, good afternoon.

4

It had been a longish day for Richardson but he had not yet finished. Coming home for a hasty meal, he hurried off immediately afterwards to visit Gosling, and – as the following extract from the *Samarai* file shows – the result of it confirmed what he had already told his wife – that he was expecting no joy from it.

'... On informing Walter Gosling the purpose of my visit was to learn where he had been between 6 p.m. and 8 p.m. on the evening in question, he replied he had been in his house watching the TV and asked if I required him to detail the programme he had seen. I replied this was unnecessary, such information being available from the *Radio Times* etc. I inquired if he had been alone while watching the TV, and Mrs Katherine Gosling, being present in the room, answered on his behalf, 'No, he was not alone. I was with him except when I went to the kitchen to prepare the supper which we ate together at this table while watching the TV.'

Those had been her actual words, and while transcribing them in his car shortly afterwards it was only the restraint due to a policeman's notebook which deterred him from adding they had been uttered with such vehemence that he half expected her to end them with, 'So leave him alone and clear out!'

5

(November 2 & 3)

Bird, a widower, had also been working late that evening. Having recorded the answers given by Williams and George the barman to every question they had been asked, he tabulated a number of them and compared them one by one.

It doesn't quite add up, he thought, slightly puzzled. In George the barman's answers he found no definite help at all, and while having no reason to doubt Williams's veracity he resolved as a first step to corroborate those of his answers which in effect amounted to an alibi. Corroboration could be obtained quickly and easily, he believed, and he decided to go and get it in the morning ... And after that? ... Frankly he did not yet know but he guessed that Williams, at the same time an eccentric and as an ex-master mariner also an educated and presumably responsible man, was likely to prove a particularly difficult customer ... He sighed, turned on the radio for the time signal and the news, and after his usual nightcap of a whisky and soda went off early to bed.

Thus after breakfast next morning he drove for the second time to Egerton Park, on this occasion for the purpose of questioning Mrs Williams not in Williams's presence. As it happened the field was clear because Williams, often an early riser, had already gone off to Liverpool to see his stamp dealer and get his hair cut.

Mrs Williams, he thought, seemed flattered rather than put out when he told her who he was, and though less affable an interviewer than Richardson he framed his first question nicely enough. 'I understand on the evening of Tuesday of last week you'd only just returned home after having been away, and in consequence you didn't want to go with Captain Williams to the Great Eastern for a drink when he went there about half-past six?'

'Who's been telling you all that?'

'He did.'

'Then he's all mixed up. I wasn't back here at half-past six, the train I was on hadn't reached Rock Ferry by then.'

'Then at what time did you arrive back in this house?'

'Let me think ... I took a taxi from the station. It would be about a quarter-past seven.'

'Was Captain Williams in when you arrived?'

'No one was in. The house was shut up and in darkness.'

'You had to let yourself in?'

'Of course. I had my key, hadn't I?'

'Are you sure the house was empty?'

'Of course I'm sure. And a nice mess I found on the dining-room carpet, all wet as if someone had spilled a

can still see the polish it lifted and the ring it made.'
drink on it. And a brandy bottle left on the table, you

'At what time that evening did Captain Williams come back?'

'Hey, why are you asking all these questions? What are you getting at?'

'All I want is to arrive at the truth.'

'Well, I'm telling you the truth. Has my old man been up to something? He's been crazy enough since his ship went aground and I wouldn't put it past him.'

'I can't answer that because I don't know yet. I'm asking questions because I'm trying to find out. And, believe me, it's in everyone's interests, Captain Williams included, that I do find out.'

'I believe you all right.' Mrs Williams's voice was bitter. 'Did he tell you I'd left him because of his craziness?'

'He didn't tell me anything about that.'

'Well, I'm telling you now. And I came back because with all his faults he's better than most. And now get on with your questions.'

'I was asking you at what time he returned here on the evening we're talking about.'

'After I'd been here about an hour. That would make it about eight or just after.'

'Was he alone when he came back?'

'No, a chap was with him. The chap who was driving him.'

'Captain Williams came in a car? His own car?'

'I thought at first it was, it looked just like it. But it wasn't. It was the chap's.'

'Do you happen to know the registration letters and number of Captain Williams's car?'

'You surely don't expect me to know a silly thing like that. It's standing in the garage if you really want them.'

Bird nodded and continued, 'Did the person who drove him back come into the house?'

'No, he just dropped my old man and turned round and drove away.'

'Did you recognize the driver of the car?'

'How could I? He never got out.'

'Have you seen that same car here before?'

'No. It was just like the Captain's as I've told you.'

'How were you able to see all this in the dark?'

'From my bedroom window of course. How else do you think?'

'When Captain Williams came in did he tell you where he'd been and who he'd been with?'

'He only said he'd been to the Great Eastern with a friend.'

'Did you ask him who the friend was?'

'I may have done but he didn't tell me. You don't know my old man, he tells me nothing he doesn't want to.'

'You say you'd come back after having left him. How long had you been away?'

'A week. But does that matter?'

'Had you written or telephoned to say you were returning?'

'Of course not, I just came. Isn't the house mine as much as his?'

'So you came back unexpectedly after having been away for a week?'

'I've already told you that.'

'Was Captain Williams surprised to see you?'

'He didn't say so.'

'Did he explain either then or later the spill on the dining-room carpet, or the brandy bottle on the table and the stain you say it made?'

'Not he.'

'Did you tell him you'd noticed both these things?'

'Of course I told him. Wouldn't you have told him?'

'And in spite of being told he gave no explanation?'

'How many more times do you want me to tell you the same thing? I've said he didn't.'

'One more question, Mrs Williams, and please think carefully before answering. Are you quite sure you and he didn't then go together to the Great Eastern that evening?'

'I'm bloody sure we didn't. He never asked me. He said he'd already been there with his friend. And the mean bastard wouldn't even 've given me a drink if I hadn't said I was dying for one. With the brandy bottle sitting there on the table too. Pour it out for yourself and give me one, he said ... And between you and me he looked as if he could do with it.'

'Thank you for having been so frank with me, Mrs Williams.'

'Too bloody frank if you ask me. And don't you go and put my old man in the nick, he's too old for it and wouldn't like it any more than I would. He may be a proper old stoat but there's many a stoat a lot worse than him.'

It's a breakthrough all right though there's quite a lot I don't yet understand, Bird thought as he drove away ... And won't Bob Richardson be pleased? Much more so than me in fact – here he was thinking of the files and messages accumulating on his office desk since Tuesday evening ... Better get back there quick and see what's happening. And not phone Bob till after lunch – the moment he hears he'll want to go at once to question Williams and he's bound to want me with him ... But I'll tell him Williams is much better left till after we get the lab report, we'll be on firmer ground then and no longer guessing. So I'll ring him during the afternoon and in the meantime God forbid any more of this *Samarai* stuff cropping up this side of the week-end – oh, to hell with the traffic-light, the whole county's getting riddled with the damned things.

CHAPTER XIII

1

The average citizen is probably unaware of how greatly the police rely upon the general public for information – though sometimes the enthusiasm with which the individual policeman accepts it may not be instantly apparent.

On the evening of the previous day – the day of the inquest and of all the subsequent activities of Bird and Richardson – a respected householder from Ness named Billy Lloyd, a man getting on in years and a self-employed plumber by trade, called at Neston police station puffing his pipe and said to the constable in the office that he and his wife had just been reading about Hartley's inquest in that evening's *Echo* and after talking it over together they'd agreed he'd best come along and report what he had seen.

'Seen about what?' the constable inquired, parking his cigarette under the counter.

Mr Lloyd knocked out his pipe and said wasn't that exactly what he'd come to tell him? In returning home from a job in Thornton Hough on the evening of Sir Henry's death, he went on, he'd driven his Morris van past two stationary cars drawn up fairly close behind each other in the short cut by the Lydiate. The time was after seven, perhaps twenty past to be more exact, and he wouldn't have thought twice about them if he hadn't fancied the front car was either Sir Henry's or one as like it as two peas, he knowing Sir Henry's grey Mercedes well enough through working at times at the Old Hall.

The constable now asked questions, to which Mr Lloyd replied he hadn't been able to see inside either of them, as a matter of fact in passing them in the dark on a narrowish road he hadn't tried to look. No, no one was standing outside either, he was positive about that. Nor could he say for certain if they had their lights on – wait a minute, the rearlights of the back one must have been on or he'd have noticed it because even nowadays loving couples in unfrequented by-ways have some respect for the law. Yes, both cars were definitely on the road, he'd have stopped if either of them had been off it or through the fence. The back car was a darkish saloon of medium size, he couldn't give a better description than that because as previously mentioned he wouldn't have taken any notice of either unless he'd thought the front one was Sir Henry's.

The duty constable, whether or not appreciating the significance of what he had been told, was a well-trained young policeman and said he was obliged for the information and would the informant now sit down beside him and repeat what he had said so that it could be written down in the form of a statement which he would then be required to sign.

Though now due to attend a Horticultural Society meeting at the Oddfellows' Hall on chrysanths and indoor tomatoes, Mr Lloyd said he would do what was asked, and in due course his statement was read back to him and signed. And there the matter did not end because no sooner had he gone than the constable went next door to show it to the sergeant, who lost no time in telephoning its gist to headquarters in Chester, promising to forward the actual document first thing in the morning.

Thus both the phone message and the statement were waiting on Bird's desk when he returned from questioning Mrs Williams in Rock Ferry, and within minutes he had put out an urgent and personal inquiry to the County Licensing authority. Moreover, being known there as a highly-placed policeman, he was favoured with an almost immediate reply.

Next, having dismissed all thoughts of lunch, he phoned Richardson in high spirits and said, 'I've had two breakthroughs for you in the past couple of hours, and you'll agree that isn't bad going even by Cheshire standards. But before telling you about them I want a description of your pilot's car as soon as you can get it.'

'I saw it at his place the other day and you can have it now. It's a dark green Ford saloon of medium size with fancy discs on its wheels and its registration number's –

'Thanks, I don't want its number, only its type and colour, and you'll be glad to know Mrs Williams wasn't lying. You'll also be interested to hear Williams has a dark green Ford saloon of medium size too. But I can't say if its wheels have fancy discs – '

'Stop being funny. I'm not with you.'

'I didn't think you would be. Look, Bob, come over here soon as possible and I'll put you in the picture, sorry I've too much on my desk here to come out anywhere and meet you. And when you've heard the story I'm sure you'll agree with me all we need do now is wait for the lab report on the seats and carpets. I'd better tell you my chaps dusted the car inside and out for prints but didn't get anything very good. That's all for now and I'll be seeing you.'

'You will. Inside an hour.'

'In the meantime you'd better make sure your pilot doesn't skip.'

Richardson laughed. 'That's already taken care of,

I've two men keeping track of all his movements. How about Williams?'

'You'll have to take a chance on him, Bob. We're poor in Cheshire and never have the spare men you always seem to have in Liverpool.'

2

(November 7)

Signed by one of its scientists, the report from the Home Office Forensic Laboratory at Preston reached police headquarters in Chester on Monday morning. 'The lab report's come in,' Bird told Richardson, phoning him at once. 'Like to meet at the Woodside Hotel in Birkenhead at twelve thirty?'

'I'll be there.'

So they sat in the saloon bar, where Bird opened his bag and Richardson read the report silently handed to him:

A front floor-carpet of a motorcar (labelled RK 1) and 2 leather-upholstered front seats of a motorcar (labelled RK 2 and RK 3 respectively) have been received from D.I. Bird of Cheshire CID, and on examination numerous fragments of newsprint (over 30) and smears of printing ink (about 20) were found on the surface of the floor carpet.

Wool fibres (about 25) of different kinds were found on the leather upholstery of both seats.

A damaged driving-mirror (labelled RK 4) was received from the same source, and about 20 fragments and numerous smaller particles of mirror-glass indistinguishable from the mirror-glass remaining in

the control were found on the surface of carpet RK 1
and on the leather surface of RK 2 and RK 3.

'So they'd put down newspapers to keep the carpets
clean,' Richardson commented, and Bird nodded.

During the discussion which followed Richardson said
what astounded him most and kept astounding him
throughout the week-end was that Williams must be
bent too. 'And wherever Hartley died – in Williams's
own house as likely as not – Williams must have been
helped to put the body in the car. And then been helped
to plant the car beside the Lydiate. A man of his size
and age couldn't have handled a heavy corpse and set it
up single-handed. Anyhow we now know there were two
cars, therefore two drivers. Presumably Gosling and
Williams.'

Bird said, 'I'm with you over most of that.'

Richardson went on, 'I spent an hour yesterday at
the pilotage office being quietly shown the actual tran-
script of evidence given by Williams at the inquiry, and
I'm now beginning to wonder if he wasn't paid to keep
away from the bridge at the material time to enable
Gosling to wreck the ship undisturbed.'

To this Bird wryly replied that being no sailor he
preferred not to commit himself about what had or
hadn't happened on board the *Samarai*. 'All that con-
cerns me personally is what happened much nearer
home. On the face of it both men were in it together,
each trying to cover the other and at the same time
cover themselves. So what we've now got to find out is
which of them did in Hartley.'

'But the pathologist said categorically he died of heart
failure,' Richardson objected.

'Quite. But he didn't explain the laceration. Said he
couldn't in fact. Probably one of them hit him with

something first. And when he so inconveniently died they must have decided the safest thing to do from their point of view was to put his body in his car and drive it away to where they staged the accident.'

'Could be. Though to me the idea of the pair of them putting their necks out to risk being charged with manslaughter – perhaps even murder – on top of everything else doesn't make sense.'

'Hadn't we better stop speculating? Once we've had their clothing examined we'll know more than enough to get the truth out of both of them. How soon can you get hold of Gosling's?'

'I'll go for it this afternoon.'

'Send it over today if you can. On my way back I'll collect Hartley's as well as Williams's and the whole lot had better go to Preston together.'

On his way home Bird paid his third visit to Egerton Park; the door was opened by Williams who began, 'I have heard of your visit here last Thursday during my absence and I am pleased to see you today – '

Being in a hurry Bird cut him short, saying formally, 'I've come to tell you certain fibres and other items have been found in the interior of Sir Henry Hartley's car and I wish to send the overcoat and jacket and trousers and shoes you were wearing on the evening of his death to a laboratory for forensic examination.'

Williams did not seem in the least perturbed. 'The suit you ask for is the one I have on now and I'll go upstairs and change it. But I have only the one overcoat and not yet being used to English winters I would like it returned quickly.'

'If the results are negative you'll have everything back within a week but if positive results are found you'll be without them for some time. In case of need I daresay we could provide you with another overcoat.'

'I am not yet as hard up as that,' Williams said, and went up to change. He came back with all the articles Bird had specified.

'Are these what you were wearing on the evening in question?' Bird spoke formally again.

'You have my word that they are.'

'Then I'll give you a receipt ... And remember there's no need for you to worry provided you're in the clear.'

'I have no worry because I *am* in the clear. When you stopped me I was about to tell you I have always been on your side.'

3

Gosling wasn't nearly so helpful, Richardson told Bird when next they met.

'What the hell have you come for now?' Gosling had asked him when he arrived.

'Everything you were wearing on the night of Hartley's death. Overcoat, jacket, trousers, shoes. The lot.'

'In aid of what?'

'For forensic examination. To compare with fibres and other things found inside Hartley's car.'

'What other things?'

'I can't tell you that.'

'What if I won't hand them over?'

'I'd draw my own conclusions.'

'I bet you'd do that. What powers have you to make me?'

'None.'

'Then you've a bloody nerve asking for them. The

trouble with you chaps is that you always want things your own way and I'm having my solicitor here first.'

'I'm glad of that – I'm sure he'll advise you to do as I ask. Provided you tell him the inquest was adjourned, also that for all I know this could turn into a murder inquiry.'

'Don't try waving your big stick at me. He wasn't murdered, I know that.'

'Then what have you to lose by giving me your clothes?'

'I'm not telling you a thing. What my wife and I don't like about you is the way you come here asking questions. And now you demand things without a warrant.'

'I'm demanding nothing, I'm merely inviting you to co-operate. And now let's cut the cackle, it isn't helping either of us. Are you or are you not giving me your clothes? And if you want your solicitor present, phone him now and be sure to tell him you haven't been charged. I don't mind waiting.'

Gosling reflected. 'If I do let you have them, how soon do I get them back?' he asked. 'And what if they're damaged?'

'They won't be damaged and the time they're kept depends entirely on what's found.'

Gosling seemed to be trying to make up his mind. 'You'll have to wait while I talk to my wife,' he then said, and left Richardson in the hall as he disappeared into the kitchen.

Before very long the kitchen door opened and Mrs Gosling came out alone; she had been crying, Richardson saw. Though pale and tense she kept control of herself and said with no more emotion than if addressing a man from the Pru, 'My husband's told me what you've come for and he's going to do what you ask. You can wait in the lounge while he gets them.'

Some minutes later Gosling entered with a bundle of clothes and a raincoat under his arm. 'Here's the lot,' he said. 'And now go.'

'If you're sure they're what you were wearing on the afternoon and evening of Hartley's death I'll give you a receipt for them.'

'Of course I'm sure.' Gosling forced a laugh. 'Do you take me for a ruddy nitwit too?'

4

With so many articles to be tested the lab report was not expected till the end of the week, and in the meantime Bird and Richardson had other fish to fry. The *Samarai* pan thus stood simmering unattended on the hob till the Wednesday morning when Richardson found time to give it a stir, and with an hour to spare he went to India Buildings to see Miss Webb.

This was his second visit since Sir Henry's death, and by now they were quite on terms. He told her she was looking a lot better than on the previous occasion; she said how shocked she had been by the adjournment of the inquest and could not understand why. 'What have you come for this time?' she then asked. 'More information about Sir Henry?'

'No, nothing about him. Only some about Williams.'

'Williams?' she echoed in surprise. 'Surely *he's* not a suspect now?'

'Don't ask,' Richardson said with a smile. 'You may be too.'

Quickly and efficiently she confirmed from her engagement book that early one afternoon three weeks previously – the afternoon of Sir Henry's departure for Hamburg, she added – Williams had come to the office without an appointment and after waiting till Sir Henry returned from lunch went in to see him and remained eleven minutes. The subject of his visit, so he'd said, was in connection with his pension and he seemed quite cheerful for once.

Richardson was equally cheerful. 'Thanks a lot. That's about all I wanted to know.'

'Won't you tell me why you're inquiring about him?'

'Oh, only routine. Just checking something for a Cheshire friend of mine.'

'You policemen never give much away, do you? ... I suppose you know all sorts of rumours are flying about the office?'

'What sort of rumours?'

'Oh, only routine ones.'

Richardson laughed and waved his notebook in her face. 'Won't you tell me? They'd go down in here, you know.'

'Then write, "Was the *Samarai* wrecked on purpose?" '

'Tell me another, that one's in already.'

On his way out through the main corridor he chanced to run into Captain Beecher who, recognizing him at once, switched his scowl into a smile. 'How's the good work going, hey?' he asked.

'Not too badly, thanks.'

'Not solved yet?' His eyebrows rose in mock surprise.

'No, not quite.'

'And never will be.' Beecher was serious now. 'I know the answer as well as you do. But with Sir Henry gone no one will ever prove it. And between you and me Armstrong of the pilotage thinks the same way.'

'I guessed that a bit ago. But tell him from me to keep his fingers crossed. And keep yours crossed too.'

(November 12)

The laboratory report, a lengthier and more formal document than the first one, was received by Bird on the Saturday morning, and after studying its contents he telephoned them at once to Richardson:

I am a Bachelor of Science and I have received from D-I Bird the following articles labelled:

RK 5   Dark brown woollen overcoat, pair of brown woollen trousers, brown woollen jacket, pair of brown shoes, from IFOR WILLIAMS.

RK 6   Blue raincoat, pair of grey woollen & nylon trousers, grey woollen jacket, pair of black shoes, from WALTER GOSLING.

RK 7   Black fine woollen overcoat, pair of black & white pin-stripe woollen trousers, pin-stripe woollen jacket, pair of patent-leather shoes, from HENRY HARTLEY.

I have examined these articles. The overcoat of RK 5 contained fibres indistinguishable from the 3 control fibres taken previously from front edge of leather upholstery of (near) seat RK 2. Fragments of newsprint (4) and traces of printing ink (about 8) adhering to the soles of brown shoes were indistinguishable from the control fragments of newsprint and control smears of printing ink taken previously from the surface of floor carpet RK 1.

No resemblance was found between control fibres

taken previously from the leather upholstery of seats RK 2 and RK 3 and the fibres contained in the articles of clothing of RK 6, and no fragments of newsprint or traces of printing ink were found adhering to the soles of RK 6 black shoes.

The jacket and trousers of RK 7 contained fibres indistinguishable from the control fibres (about 12) taken previously from the seating area of the leather upholstery of seats RK 2 and RK 3. No fragments of newsprint were found adhering to the soles of patent-leather shoes, but a slight trace of printing ink found on the narrow front edge of sole of left-foot shoe was indistinguishable from the control smears of printing ink taken previously from floor carpet RK 1.

Numerous fragments (about 20) and particles (about 100) of mirror glass indistinguishable from the control fragments and particles taken previously from floor carpet RK 1 and damaged driving-mirror RK 4 were found on the overcoat and trouser turn-ups and brown shoes of RK 5, and on the jacket, trousers, and patent-leather shoes of RK 7. No fragments or particles of mirror glass were found on any of the articles of clothing or shoes labelled RK 6.

This Statement is true to the best of my knowledge and I make it knowing that, if it is tendered in evidence, I shall be liable to prosecution if I have wilfully stated in it anything which I know to be false and do not believe to be true.

'So that's it,' Richardson said, and went on, 'Your chap first? He's likely to be more forthcoming than mine.'

Bird agreed, and they arranged to meet in an hour's time at the entrance to Egerton Park, and as soon as Richardson rang off Bird phoned the station officer at

Bromborough police station and told him what he would be wanting.

'Everything will be ready for you, sir,' the station officer assured him.

CHAPTER XIV

(November 12)

1

They reached Egerton Park at much the same time, parked their cars outside Williams's house, and Bird rang the bell. The door was opened by Mrs Williams who stared at Richardson, greeted Bird with a winning smile, and said, 'He's in what he calls his study and doing his blessed stamps if you want to speak to him.'

Bird said they did, and she opened the dining-room door. Inside they saw Williams as yet undisturbed and seated at the table. Before he could say a word Bird, addressing him in the kind of formal police-language which made Richardson feel he wanted to look the other way, said, 'As a result of the laboratory examination of your clothing I have certain questions to ask you and I wish to question you further regarding some of your answers to my questions on Wednesday the 2nd. The police station at Bromborough is a convenient place for this, and I invite you to accompany us there at once.'

Williams retorted, 'Not so convenient for me,' and put away his stamp-tweezers in their little box. 'But when I have locked my safe and told Mrs Williams where I am going I am willing to accompany you.'

Little was said during the brief drive to the police station, and on arrival Bird conducted Richardson and Williams through the main doors into the interviewing room. There, according to instructions, a constable was already sitting at the smaller table. He was waiting to record every word of what would shortly be said, and he stood up as they entered.

Motioning Williams to sit on the hard chair opposite him, Bird at once told him he was not compelled to say anything but that if he did what he said would be written down and used in evidence. Williams nodded without speaking, and Bird let off his first question:

'When I asked you where you were between 6 p.m. and 8 p.m. on the day of Hartley's death you told me you were in your house until about 6.30 and then you went to the Great Eastern for a drink. Did you say that?'

'I believe I did.'

'When you returned home was Mrs Williams there?'

'She was.'

'I have reason to believe you were brought home by a friend who didn't come indoors with you?'

'That is so.'

'In a car?'

'Yes.'

'His car not yours?'

'Yes.'

'Was the name of your friend Walter Gosling?'

'It was.'

'Had he been to the Great Eastern with you?'

'No.'

'Had you yourself in fact been to the Great Eastern that evening?'

'No.'

'Then where had you and Walter Gosling been?'

'I will tell you all about it. But here in this room I feel rather confused and do not quite know where to begin.'

Richardson glanced at Bird who nodded, and Richardson said to Williams, 'Let's start at the beginning. There's no need to go back to the time when your ship was wrecked, we know how you felt about that. We understand you went to see Hartley in his office on the afternoon of October 18 just before he left for Hamburg, also that you told Miss Webb the purpose of your visit was to speak to him about your pension. Is that correct?'

'It is.'

'During your conversation with him was the *Samarai* mentioned by either of you?'

'No, it was not.'

'Did you talk to him about anything other than your pension?'

'No.'

'What did he say to you about it?'

'That he would do his best to obtain from the trustees the increase for which I was asking. It was a question of the interpretation of the Pension Fund rules, and he agreed with me.'

'So it was an amicable meeting in every way?'

'Absolutely.'

'What did you do after you left Sir Henry?'

'I went to Broadhurst Drive to speak to Mr Gosling.'

'To speak about what?'

'The *Samarai*.'

'What did you say to him about the *Samarai*?'

'That I had been to Sir Henry and now I knew the truth about the loss of my ship.'

'What truth was that?'

'That she had been grounded deliberately.'

'How did he react when you told him that?'

'He said he did not know what I was talking about.'

'And then?'

'I told him I had learned something important which was not made known to the Pilotage Committee and he had made a slip.'

'What did he say to that?'

'He told me I was talking nonsense. Bloody nonsense was what he said.'

'He still didn't believe you?'

'No. But perhaps he was beginning to, because he invited me indoors. I think it was the slip which was worrying him and he wanted to find out what it was.'

'You went indoors with him?'

'Yes.'

'And then?'

'I reminded him about his pipe.'

'His *pipe*? What's his pipe got to do with it?'

'I will explain.' Williams took a folded piece of paper from his breast pocket and unfolded it. 'Mr Donovan the Quartermaster told me this when I spoke to him after the inquiry in the Company office was over and I wrote it down at once. I will read you his exact words:

As soon as he first tells me to give her more port I see him stoop down under the dodger* to light his pipe. I know his first match goes out because I hear him swear. When at last it is lit he bobs up and sees we're still running close to the starboard-hand buoy. 'Christ, give her more port!' he shouts at me. I'm no Christ but I do what he says and of course the ship sheers off to port, and when he orders Hard a starboard she answers perfect but too late.

'That was Gosling's slip?' Richardson asked.

'Yes.'

'Enough to convince you he deliberately wrecked your ship?'

'Of course.'

'Were you not convinced long before you knew anything about what you've just read to us?' Bird put in.

* Seafaring term for the canvas weather-cloth secured to the bridge rail to give protection against wind and weather.

'I have always been convinced.'

'What did Gosling say next?' Richardson resumed.

'Nothing. But I now knew he knew I knew the truth.'

'What happened next?'

'I told him how Sir Henry, never a man to give away money for nothing, was so interested when he heard what Mr Donovan had seen that he offered at once to increase my pension.'

'Had you in fact read or shown to Sir Henry what you've just read to us?'

'No, I have already told you we did not discuss the *Samarai* at all.'

'In other words you were trying to bluff Gosling?'

'You may put it that way if you wish. But he did not think it bluff. Neither did I.'

'And next?'

'I told him if he doubted my word he could telephone to Sir Henry. I think at first he intended to, but he changed his mind.'

'What if he had?'

Williams chuckled. 'I was on safe ground there. Had I not seen Sir Henry's bag in the corner of his room and the air-travel tickets on his desk? And after my conversation with Sir Henry had not Miss Webb told me he was leaving the office almost immediately to go to London for his aeroplane?'

'What after that?'

'Mr Gosling asked me why I had come and what exactly I was after. I was expecting that and prepared for it too.'

'What did you reply?'

'I told him I felt sure that whatever reward he had received for what he did was not enough, and that by carrying out the wishes of an evil man he had been reduced to Third Class pilot in his prime of life and I had become a pensioner, and did we not therefore owe it to ourselves to put our heads together and persuade Sir Henry to treat us more generously?'

Bird intervened. 'You suggested to Gosling you and he should conspire to demand money with menaces from Sir Henry Hartley?'

'Exactly. But I have already told you I am on your side, and you gentlemen will understand it was part of my plan to bring Sir Henry to justice.'

'How did Gosling react?' Richardson asked.

'At first he seemed very surprised and then he said he thought there was a lot in what I had said but he would need a few days to think it over. I agreed to that because I was expecting it, but said he must not think it over for too long or my patience would become exhausted and I would inform the police. Between you and me I felt certain he was intending to go and tell Sir Henry and obtain his advice.'

'What happened then?'

Williams chuckled again. 'I had scared him so much that he offered me a drink.'

The tension suddenly relaxed by Williams's unexpected reply, Bird glanced at Richardson and the constable at the table and said, 'We could all do with a break for a few minutes and I'll send to the canteen for cups of tea before Captain Williams tells us the rest.'

'I could do with something stronger than tea,' Williams sighed.

'You won't get anything stronger than tea here,' Bird told him.

'It's the same in Liverpool,' Richardson said. 'The Home Office won't stand for it.'

Once the teacups had been cleared away and the writer was back at his table Bird asked Williams, 'How did you come to think by demanding money with menaces from Sir Henry you could bring him to justice?'

'I was needing evidence of course, I have not come to that part of my plan yet.'

'Then tell us what you or Gosling did next.'

'The next move was of course Mr Gosling's. He telephoned some days later and said he had decided to join in and thought the best way to negotiate with Sir Henry would be for the three of us to get together. I felt sure he was now acting on Sir Henry's instructions since he had waited till Sir Henry had returned from Hamburg. I told him I was agreeable, and we discussed where the meeting was to take place. Mr Gosling said his own house was out of the question and Sir Henry would not care for a public house, and when I suggested my house Mr Gosling said that would be all right provided Mrs Williams was out of the way while the meeting was taking place. I told him this presented no difficulty since she happened to be away on a visit to friends, and Mr Gosling then said it would best be arranged for a time when Sir Henry was on his way home from the office and suggested six o'clock on the coming Tuesday.'

'Do you mean Tuesday the 25th?'

'I think that was the date.'

'In fact the day Hartley died?'

Williams nodded. 'It turned out that way.'

'So the meeting took place as arranged?'

'Yes. In my dining-room.'

'Did Hartley and Gosling arrive together?'

'No. Separately.'

'What happened at the meeting?'

'I will tell you. Being in my house I acted as chairman and after welcoming Sir Henry I told him the wrecking of the *Samarai* had brought considerable financial hardship both to Mr Gosling and myself. Mr Gosling's career and future prospects had been ruined, and by having lost my livelihood several years before my expected retiring age I had difficulty in adjusting myself to such sudden loss of employment as well as to the straitened circumstances which accompanied it.'

'Did Gosling know you were going to say this?'

'No. I had told him previously to leave the talking to me and all he had to do was to keep his mouth shut.'

'What did Hartley reply?'

'He just said he knew all that and told me to get on with it.'

'Go on then.'

'I can tell you exactly what I said to Sir Henry because I memorized it beforehand and have not yet forgotten it. I said, "I do not ask you what you have done for Mr Gosling in the way of a reward because that is not my business. In the apparent circumstances of my own case I must concede you have not treated me harshly as regards my pension. But I use the word 'apparent' since circumstances are not always as they appear to be. I am a direct man and you must excuse me for speaking directly. Mr Gosling and I both felt the recompense each of us has so far received is inadequate. Speaking for myself, I am not greedy. All I ask for is one thousand pounds, to enable me to increase my pension by purchasing an annuity, and I do not press you for immediate payment. But unhappily I am short of ready cash to meet current expenses and need twenty-five pounds of it at once. If you have your cheque book with you I will of course accept a cheque, otherwise I will call at your office tomorrow morning to collect five five-pound notes."'

'How did Hartley react?'

'He said he had never before had to deal with a blackmailer and would I first tell him what actual evidence I had, and when I said I objected to the word "blackmailer" he said he was not there to discuss verbal niceties and I must answer his question. I answered it by saying I considered the presence of Mr Gosling more than sufficient evidence.'

'What did he say to that?'

'He reminded me I had just told him circumstances were not always what they appeared to be and might I not be forming the wrong conclusion myself? He then said in a situation such as this he understood it was customary for the intended victim, assuming he was disposed to meet the initial demand, to inquire of the blackmailer what security he was being offered with respect to the future. I replied by assuring him I was a man of integrity and principle and any further security he was seeking could only be found in his own conscience.'

'Did that satisfy him?'

'He did not say. He just said he thought my demand for only one thousand pounds was on the modest side and what was I going to do if he refused to meet it? I said this seemed to me a hypothetical question because while I had always looked upon him as a man of courage I did not think even he had sufficient courage to take the consequences of refusing.'

'How did he reply to that?'

'He said courage did not enter into it, this seeming to him a matter merely requiring common sense, and if I was relying on Mr Gosling for my evidence what if he proved a broken reed? I said that of course remained to be seen and in any event it would be unwise of him to imagine I had no further evidence.'

'Did he ask what the further evidence was?'

'No, he just laughed and said if I believe the *Samarai* was wrecked on purpose it was up to me to prove it either with or without Mr Gosling's help and in his opinion I was either a criminal or a lunatic, he had not yet decided which. And I could now have his answer, which was final – I would get nothing from him, not even a penny. Getting up from his chair he then ordered Mr Gosling to accompany him out of my house.'

'So that was the end of the meeting?' Bird asked, hoping against hope the climax was at last approaching.

'No, not quite. Because Mr Gosling spoke up and said, "We can't leave it like this. After all he thinks he's got some justification." That made Sir Henry so angry that he almost shouted, "Justification for what? For blackmailing me?" To quieten him I said that asking for fair compensation for a wicked deed done at the expense of Mr Gosling and myself could hardly be called blackmail.'

'Quite a point,' Richardson said in sly aside to Bird who frowned and nodded to Williams to go on.

'By now Sir Henry had lost his temper and after telling me Mr Gosling knew on which side his bread was buttered and to leave him out of it he told Mr Gosling he wanted no further interruptions from him. He then shouted at me I was a crazy Welshman and could go ahead and be damned to me.'

'What did you say to that?' Richardson asked.

'I told him in the eyes of God he was damned already, and when I said that he pushed his chair aside and came towards me in such a threatening manner that I felt sure he was going to strike me. Not wanting any disturbance in my dining-room I retreated towards the door where he could not reach me, Mr Gosling having placed himself between us. Still shouting, Sir Henry told me over Mr Gosling's shoulder I now knew exactly where I stood and that his last words to me were No, No, No. And curiously enough those were indeed his last words. His shouting faded away and he clutched at his chest and his body became rigid and he toppled over and fell to the floor like a dropped sack of grain. As he fell his head caught the edge of my sideboard.'

'Got all that?' Richardson inquired of the busily-writing constable.

'Nearly but not quite, sir ... I have now.'

'Go on,' Richardson told Williams. 'And not so fast.'

'I was very upset and I could not resist watching the blood oozing from Sir Henry's head over my carpet when Mr Gosling said, "Where's your brandy, Captain? Get it quick." At first I could not think where it was and then I remembered it was in the corner cupboard and I hurried to get it. Mr Gosling then poured out not quite half a tumblerful into the pewter beer mug standing on the sideboard and knelt beside Sir Henry and lifted his head and tried to administer it. "I can't make him take any," he said to me, and I went to my telephone on the table in the window to summon the doctor. The operator answered at once but the number I wanted was engaged. While I was doing this Mr Gosling called out he thought Sir Henry had stopped breathing and he could not feel any pulse. I too knelt beside him, and when I told Mr Gosling I could not feel it either he said, "Christ, he must be dead." I told him I had never seen a man die so quickly and that the sooner the doctor arrived the better, and I was at the telephone to try the number again when Mr Gosling called to me to lay off because no doctor would be any good to him now and seeing all the blood on the carpet the doctor would be sure to send for the police and we must now think of ourselves.

'I said that was exactly what I was doing, but Mr Gosling said once the police came into it we were finished because how could we explain the three of us in my dining-room? I said I had nothing to fear by telling the truth, and he said he would tell the truth too – that Sir Henry had a heart attack and died because I was blackmailing him. I said that was only a very small part of the truth, and Mr Gosling drank all the brandy he had poured out for Sir Henry and said, "Whether you like it or not we're both in this together so for God's sake keep quiet a minute and let me do some thinking."

'I did as he said but not because he told me to. I was thinking Sir Henry's death was a true manifestation of the power of God and the way in which His hand had struck him down was a lesson to all evil-doers, Mr Gosling included. I was also thinking it was awkward of Him to have chosen my dining-room as the place of Sir Henry's doom, and I had almost made up my mind to insist on having the doctor, the police too if he demanded it, when Mr Gosling suddenly said, "I've got it! But we'll have to be pretty quick about it, and thank God living where you do no one can see us."

'When I asked what he suggested he said, "We'll put him in his car and I'll drive it half way to his home and ditch it. I know the place all right. But I won't be able to set him up in his driving seat single-handed so you'll have to come too. In fact we'll need two cars because I'll want bringing back. But first get some cold water and we'll wash the blood off the side of his head and clean up your carpet." '

'What did you think about all that?' Bird inquired, grim-faced and unfriendly.

'I was very relieved because it was a way of getting rid of the body quickly and without any publicity, and I told Mr Gosling he was cleverer than I thought and no wonder he had made such a good job of the *Samarai*. He was getting his gloves from the hall and telling me to put on mine too, and we carried Sir Henry out of the house, Mr Gosling holding him by his shoulders and I took his legs. He was much heavier than I expected, and not being used to walking backwards in the dark I stumbled once or twice. But being a pilot Mr Gosling had good night-vision and managed all right. Sir Henry kept toppling over while we were trying to stow him on the front seat of his car, and Mr Gosling told me to fetch some rope. Not having any, we had to do without. As soon as everything was ready Mr Gosling told me to get into his car, the same kind of Ford as mine, and follow behind him to where he was going, and when he asked me why I was laughing I said it was because first he had wrecked my ship and now he was going to wreck its owner's car.'

Here more cups of tea were asked for and supplied, and when business was resumed Captain Williams told the two detectives how on reaching their destination and after having parked the cars one behind the other Gosling spread a newspaper on the floor of the Mercedes to protect its carpet from their muddy footprints. On one occasion they had to stoop down out of sight when a van unexpectedly appeared, but it went past without stopping and did not even slacken speed. As soon as Gosling had driven the Mercedes through the fence they pushed Sir Henry across into the driving seat, propping him up to look as natural as possible, and towards the end of this operation Gosling's head accidentally caught the interior driving-mirror and smashed it.

'Mr Gosling then took me back to Rock Ferry,' Williams continued, 'and on the way I was tired and dozed off and I dreamed the *Samarai* affair was now finally closed. I told Mr Gosling this and he said I was an optimist and in his view it had hardly begun. As we turned into my gateway I noticed the lights on in several of my rooms. Mr Gosling noticed them too and said, "That's funny, I was sure we'd turned everything off." I said it was not my idea of fun as it could only mean Mrs Williams had returned, and Mr Gosling said in that event the quicker he cleared off the better. While I was getting out of his car he said, "Where have we been? I mean we'll both have to tell the same story." I suggested the Great Eastern, a public house near Rock Ferry swimming-pool, and Mr Gosling said, "O.K. and I wish to God it had been," and drove away.

'I was annoyed with Mrs Williams for having returned without notice and became even more annoyed when she began questioning me about where I had been and who with, also about the brandy bottle on the table and the wet patch on the carpet. I told her to help herself to some brandy if she wanted and to give me some too, and as I did not want further questioning I told her to go away to the kitchen and cook the supper. The rest you know yourselves.'

As yet there was no respite for Captain Williams. The silence following the end of his story was broken by Bird telling him his written statement was now required, and another hour passed while it was being dictated, read back to him, and corrected.

Borrowing a pen, Williams signed it. 'I would like to go home now if you gentlemen want nothing more,' he then said.

Bird, who had been out of the room doing his home-work while most of the statement was being made, replied, 'Not yet, you can't ... Ifor Williams, I charge you under Sections 29 and 30 of the Larceny Act of 1861 that you conspired with Walter Gosling to demand money with menaces from the late Sir Henry Hartley. I further charge you under Sections 16, 17, and 23 of the Births and Deaths Registration Act of 1953 that you failed to give information of Hartley's death to the Registrar of Births and Deaths within the prescribed period of 5 days.'

Williams had been listening carefully. 'May I go now? This is the first time I have been charged and you must pardon my ignorance.'

Bird shook his head. 'The first offence with which you're charged is serious and you have to remain in custody. On Monday you'll go before a magistrate and you can apply for bail. It's of course up to the magistrate, but we won't oppose it.'

And there, in the anomalous position of all those who are 'helping the police with their inquiries', Captain Williams may for the moment safely be left. In fairness to his hosts he was provided with a good supper, a small single room with a hard bed, and an excellent breakfast. He was also permitted to telephone to Mrs Williams, not of course in private, and she came to visit him on Sunday.

Just before departing Richardson had paid Williams a brief call in his cell. 'You've been very co-operative and I hope you'll find no one will be hard on you. Don't forget to ask for bail on Monday, and for legal aid too if you need it. My other advice is to get hold of a good solicitor as soon as you can.'

3

'We've broken it, sir,' Richardson announced late that afternoon to Chief Inspector Young at Divisional Headquarters. 'Williams has been making a statement and I've a copy with me. I've more than enough now to bring Gosling in. But only on secondary charges, and that's where I'd be glad of your advice.'

Young filled his pipe, lit it, and held out his hand. 'I'll read Williams's statement first,' he said.

STATEMENT OF WITNESS

Ifor Williams O.B.E., Egerton Park, Rock Ferry, Cheshire, pensioner and no occupation, stated age 61, says:

I make the following statement voluntarily, having been invited to do so by 2403 Detective Inspector R. Bird.

I am a retired sea captain and have held an Extra Master's Certificate for 31 years. I was employed for 37 years by the New Guinea Steamship Company of Water Street, Liverpool, and was retired in September last when my ship, the motor vessel Samarai, *was wrecked on the Mersey Revetment. I was convinced that the pilot Walter Gosling, who was in charge at the time, ran the vessel aground deliberately, and I believed he did this in return for a reward given to him by the owner of the vessel Sir Henry Hartley (deceased). About 4 weeks ago I had a conversation with Walter Gosling in his house, and having succeeded in making him believe I knew more than in fact I did....*

Reading on and puffing away at his pipe, Young made no comment till he reached Williams's account of the meeting with Sir Henry which Gosling had arranged: *I admit I demanded money from Sir Henry Hartley but I did not do so for revenge. I did it solely for the purpose of obtaining evidence which I could give to the police.*

'The motive is immaterial. He hangs himself there,' he said, and spoke next when he came to: *If I had known at the time that the police were conducting their own inquiry I would have acted differently.* 'Williams didn't know?' he asked, surprised.

'Afraid not, sir. He was low on my list for interrogation and you'll remember you thought I was starting 'flu and ordered me home the same afternoon I was going to see him. Then of course Sir Henry died, and talking to Williams seemed relatively unimportant.'

'I see. A pity all the same.'

Young spoke again on reaching: *Sir Henry refused to pay me anything, and when I asked him to reconsider his refusal he became abusive and sustained the heart attack from which he died instantly.* 'How inconvenient for them ... Do you believe what he says here, Bob?' *In falling to the ground his head struck the edge of the sideboard in my dining-room. I had not hit him or in any way caused the laceration on the side of his head.*

'I do, sir. And Bird does too. Though of course he'll check up by examining both the room and the sideboard.'

Young nodded, pausing again at: *I wished to send for the doctor but Walter Gosling dissuaded me and after some discussion I helped him to dispose of the body.* 'How stupid can a grown man be,' he muttered half to himself, and read on till: *On arriving at the place which Walter Gosling had said he knew of near Willaston he drove the car containing the body through the wooden fence, and he and I arranged the body to make it appear an accident had occurred subsequent to and as the result of a heart attack which had also occurred there.* 'They might have got away with it,' he said to Richardson.

'They might, sir. It was lucky for us the chap driving

past who saw the two cars ultimately decided to report them.'

Young had now reached the final lines of the statement: *Supporting my contention that I did not intend to retain any money received from Sir Henry Hartley I wish to say I made a full précis of the conversation I had with Walter Gosling at the time when I put forward my proposal to him. I did this with the intention of handing it to the police together with the £25 I hoped to receive from Sir Henry Hartley. The précis was compiled and typed by me on the evening of the day when the conversation took place and will be found beside the stamp albums in my safe.*

'So he's a stamp collector?' Young said, laying the statement aside. 'Once I was too, quite a nice little collection it was ... But I gave them all away to a girl friend. Before I was married of course ... This précis of his should be useful evidence but not in the way he thinks. Bird's getting it, I suppose?'

'Yes, sir. Williams gave him the key.'

Knocking out his pipe and refilling it, Young smoked reflectively for a minute or two. He then said, 'Is the man daft?'

'You'd think so, the way he's gone about things and the jam he's landed himself in. But he didn't give me that impression – in fact in most ways I'd say he's very much all there. And however fantastic it seems to you and me I really do believe he thought his mad idea of blackmailing Hartley into giving him evidence was going to work. I believe too if Hartley had been foolish enough to part he'd have brought the money straight to us.'

'A real teaser for us if he had,' Young said in his dry way.

'Yes, sir. How he could have imagined five clean or dirty fivers were going to fasten anything on Hartley beats me altogether, he must be under the delusion we're a lot more accomplished than we are. In fact I suppose you're right – from his behaviour right through the piece he must be quite daft. But when it comes to the day of reckoning we mustn't forget he's rendered us a signal service – it's him and no one else who's put Gosling in the net. Otherwise I couldn't have got near him. Though when all's said and done I've only got him nailed on comparatively minor counts, and that's where I'd like your advice.

'You see, sir, Beecher the New Guinea Company's marine super summed up the situation right a few days ago when he said to me, "I know the answer as well as you do, but no one will ever prove it." He meant of course with Sir Henry gone, but personally I don't think his death makes any difference. Here I'd better mention Williams told us how after the Company inquiry was over he learned from his Quartermaster that a few seconds before the ship ran aground Gosling bent down under the bridge rail and monkeyed about trying to light his pipe. To Williams there seemed to be tremendous significance in that. There may have been too, but to my mind not enough to sway a jury composed of landsmen, and when Bird and I were discussing it afterwards he agreed it was far from conclusive and, as he said, any defending counsel could make haywire of it. So that's why what the Quartermaster was alleged to have said doesn't appear in Williams's statement.

'Anyhow it's entirely due to Williams I've got Gosling on two counts – Conspiring with and aiding and abetting Williams to demand money with menaces and the much lesser one of Failing to register a death. But I can't get him on the one which matters – Conspiring to wreck the *Samarai*. We know all right he did, but there's no hard evidence to put before a jury. So will you agree to me trying to do a bit of horse-trading with him? You admit the *Samarai*, I'll tell him, and we won't press the Conspiring to demand money with menaces. I'd tell him too in the eyes of the law both are equally serious and that he'd be sure to go down for a long time on either of them, so what's the good of having to face two serious charges when we'd be content with one?'

'I don't like it,' Young said, shaking his head. 'I also doubt if Gosling's the type to admit to anything he knows he needn't. But what about his wife? Is she on his side? Or ours? You've said she was crying when you went for his clothes, and that means it's likely she knows the truth. Wives usually do. She can't give evidence against him, I know that, but she may be able to influence him. After all Hartley was her uncle and quite apart from him giving her a valuable house it seems they were fond of each other. For all you and I know she's got very strong feelings about it all.'

'She's certainly a stronger character than her husband and at least it's worth trying, sir.'

'All right, Bob, go off and see what you can do. And if it's any help I'll come and talk to Gosling myself when you get him inside.'

'Thanks, sir, that could be a good idea too. If he's at home I'll be bringing him in tonight.'

4

Walter Gosling, after kissing Kath and Margaret good night, put on his overcoat, picked up his bag, and closed the front door. Noting thankfully it was a fine clear evening he got into his Ford saloon, dumped his bag on the seat beside him, and switched on the ignition and lights. Garage doors and garden gates were open, and he began backing out into Broadhurst Drive. He was bound for East Brunswick to board the *Groote Schuur* and take her at high water through Brunswick Entrance into the Mersey, thence to the Bar. There, weather conditions permitting, the punt would come for him and transfer him to No 3 Pilot Boat cruising half a mile away, and as the *Groote Schuur* was a small Dutch coaster entered outwards for Amsterdam with a loaded draught of only 9 feet the amount he would earn would be about four pounds.

Gosling's intentions were temporarily thwarted by what he saw in his driving-mirror – a car with bright headlights drawn up bang across his gateway. He hooted vigorously several times but the car's driver either did not hear or was not caring. Bounding out in anger to tell him to shift, he now saw the bloody thing was a police car with a uniformed driver, and its interior light was on and beside the driver sat Richardson.

'Move your car and let me out!' Gosling shouted. 'I've a ship to board at Brunswick in twenty minutes and can't wait a moment. What have you come for anyway?'

Lowering his window Richardson answered simply, 'You.'

'I've already told you there's nothing doing! Come back tomorrow – no, make it Monday in case I'm detained at the Bar.'

'Nothing doing,' Richardson retorted. 'You go in and phone the pilotage office to send a substitute and tell them you're coming with me to the main bridewell to make a statement. My driver will do the phoning if you like.'

'Statement about what?'

'Several things, one of them being why you gave me the wrong clothes. I've brought them back and want a receipt for them.'

167

Gosling was sensible enough to realize further argument was useless. 'I'll come under protest. After I've told my wife. And she can ring the pilotage office, I'm not having any of you lot doing that.'

The porch light came on. Kath had heard the commotion and appeared in the doorway. 'What's happening?' she called. Then she saw and came running forward.

'He says I've to go with him to make a statement.'

'What, now? ...'

'So he says. Ring up the pilotage office and tell them. And bring in my bag from the car and close the garage.'

'No, you'll need your bag,' Richardson said. 'I'm sorry about this, Mrs Gosling.'

She looked at him and said, 'You needn't be.' Turning to her husband, she looked at him too. 'Walt, you'd better not forget what I've told you.'

In one of the interviewing rooms at the main bridewell Richardson merely told Gosling he'd had a good run for his money and now the time had come for him to talk. 'And remember I know about your undertaking to Williams to bring Hartley to his house, where the two of you attempted to squeeze him. And there's no need to explain why the clothes you gave me weren't the ones you'd been wearing – I know too how you got rid of the body when he died on you.'

'So old Williams has been telling you all this? ... Well, he's got his own skin to think of and I suppose I can't blame him. He's round the bend anyway and I wish I'd done what I nearly did when he came to see me – kicked his arse and told him to run away and play.'

'It mightn't have made all that difference. I'm now going to caution you, and after that you can say as much or as little as you like. And remember everything's got to be written down so don't speak too fast.'

'I've had a good run for my money, have I?' Gosling let out a laugh. 'As a matter of fact I haven't had a bloody cent ... So what with one thing and another I'm going to talk.'

STATEMENT OF WITNESS

Walter Gosling, 'Marina', Broadhurst Drive, Aigburth, Liverpool, occupation Mersey pilot, stated age 43, says:

I have been told by 1713 Detective Inspector R. L. Richardson that I need not say anything unless I wish to and that whatever I say may be given in evidence.

I have been in the Mersey pilotage service all my working life, having been a First Class pilot for 12 years. For the last 4 of these I was appropriated to the New Guinea Steamship Company of Liverpool, and in September last the MV Samarai of that Company ran aground in Crosby Channel while in my charge. She was inward bound at the time. At the subsequent inquiry I was Severely Reprimanded by the Pilotage Committee and reduced to Third Class pilot.

I expected the matter would end there but it did not, and I may as well now admit I ran the vessel aground deliberately, having been induced to do so by her owner Sir Henry Hartley K.B.E., who was the uncle of my wife Katherine Gosling. He had previously bought a house for her in Jersey and in her name, but that had nothing to do with this affair. He bought it about eight months ago because he had no family of his own and my wife was his only niece and on account of my betting habits he looked on me as being financially unsound.

I allowed myself to be bribed by him because I was short of money owing to betting losses. He had paid my betting losses on two previous occasions and had told me on the second occasion he would never do so again. Notwithstanding this I had to approach him this third time because my losses amounted to about £700, which was £700 more than I had, and I was being pressed for payment by the bookmaker concerned who had threatened to inform the Pilotage Authority if I did not pay up. Sir Henry Hartley said he would pay the £700 only if I consented to run the Samarai aground at the first favourable opportunity. At first I was very shocked by his proposal but I knew the Company was in financial difficulties and believed it would help him, also myself, if I consented to do what he asked. When the time came I did not want to do it but I felt bound by my promise, seeing that he had already enabled me to pay the bookmaker the £700.

Sir Henry Hartley had also promised me a further reward, but only on condition that the Samarai became a total loss. This reward was to compensate me by gifts of money for my loss of income as a First Class pilot, or, if dismissed from the service, to provide a suitable income for my wife and myself in her house in Jersey. He further promised on his death to bequeath to my wife sufficient money to maintain us in Jersey. His death occurred before he carried out either of these promises, and I have received nothing from him. My wife had been told she would receive a legacy of £5000 under the terms of a will he made a number of years previously, but her solicitors have now informed her his estate is likely to be insolvent.

My wife knew all about it, the Samarai I mean, because she suspected it, and in the end I thought it best to admit it to her. After my admission she had words with me about it on several occasions, and after Sir Henry's death she said she would leave me if I got away with it but would stick to me if I told the truth and accepted the punishment I deserved. That is the main reason why I am telling you the truth now.

When Captain Ifor Williams came to my house about four weeks ago I may as well admit he bluffed me into believing he had discovered a lot more about the grounding of the Samarai than I thought possible, and that was why instead of telling him to go to hell I was scared into promising him I would consider joining with him for the purpose of threatening Sir Henry into giving us more money. I made this promise in the belief it was the safest thing I could do in the circumstances, seeing that it would give me time to consult Sir Henry about this new situation and obtain his advice about how best to deal with it. Sir Henry had gone to Hamburg at the time but I informed him in his office immediately after his return, also that I had no intention of blackmailing him myself. If he was alive today he would confirm this. He told me to arrange a meeting with Williams which he said he would attend himself, and he explained his intention was to call Williams's bluff and put him in his proper place.

The meeting which I arranged took place in Williams's house the following day, and I heard Williams demand £1000. He also demanded an immediate payment of £25 which he said was for current expenses but this was not in addition to the £1000. In my opinion these demands together with the high words subsequently exchanged between them brought on the heart attack from which Sir Henry died during the meeting. I had intervened towards the end of the discussion because I believed Williams still constituted some danger to me and I considered that Sir Henry should have humoured him more than he did. I stood between them as Sir Henry moved towards Williams in an angry manner but there was definitely no physical violence, *the wound on Sir Henry's head being caused by him catching the edge of a large piece of furniture in the room as he fell. I saw this happen myself and can swear to it.*

Regarding the other matter in which I am concerned, it was necessary for me to try to conceal Sir Henry's death in Williams's house in Rock Ferry because the fact that the three of us were there together would have taken some explaining. The way I chose for disposing of his body seemed to me at the time the best solution but I now see it was a mistake.

WALTER GOSLING

I have read the above statement and have been told I may correct it or alter it or add anything I wish. I do not wish to, and the statement is true and I have made it of my own free will.

WALTER GOSLING

CHAPTER XV

1

(November 14)

Eager to find the précis in Williams's safe and to satisfy himself about the cause of the damage to Hartley's head, Inspector Bird drove to Rock Ferry early on Monday morning.

He soon accepted that Williams had been telling the truth; he could find no evidence of murder or manslaughter and did not think even a charge of causing Grievous Bodily Harm could be sustained. Traces of blood still remaining on the edge of the massive Victorian sideboard showed that proficiency with a duster was not among Mrs Williams's accomplishments as a housekeeper, and with his penknife he removed tiny particles of skin and blood from the polished surface of the wood and placed them in an envelope with scrapings of stained wool from the carpet. To support Williams's story he was intending to send them to the forensic laboratory for confirmation that the blood was human and of the same group.

An obviously distressed Mrs Williams kept hovering in the background, and while the photographers he had brought with him were taking pictures of the sideboard, the round stain on the carpet, and of the room itself, he unbent and felt a sudden urge to talk kindly to her. In all his long experience he'd never before come across a case of demanding money by menaces with so altruistic a motive, he told her, and Mrs Williams, not knowing what altruistic meant, nodded wisely and said, 'Oh yes, he's like that with his stamps too.' Bird went on to assure her that in all the circumstances it was likely Williams would be treated leniently by the courts. 'And I'll do what little I can to help him,' he promised. 'In fact he'll be coming before the Bromborough bench in half an hour and I'm getting off there now to make sure the prosecuting inspector tells the magistrates we don't object to bail.'

In readiness for a prompt start the Bromborough justices of the peace assembled in their room a few minutes beforehand. As usual their clerk had laid the day's charge sheet on the table, and he looked in to say only No 8 on the list was out of the ordinary. 'I've arranged for it to be called first in No 1 Court,' he said. 'The police will be asking for a remand and it won't take more than a couple of minutes.'

At ten o'clock precisely the six magistrates present, already assigned by their senior to one court or the other, divided themselves into two groups of three and departed from their room. The first group disappeared into No 2 Court, concerned that day only with motoring and matrimonial cases.

The second, consisting of two men and a woman, filed into No 1 Court, and as they entered the usher, a uniformed constable at that period, mumbled, 'All rise.'

The magistrates semi-bowed to the almost empty room, and everyone sat down.

'Bring up Ifor Williams,' the magistrates' clerk ordered and in an aside to the bench said, 'I understand he's been in custody since Saturday.'

Williams went into the dock and the clerk said to him, 'Ifor Williams, you are charged under Sections 29 and 30 of the Larceny Act of 1861 that you conspired to demand money with menaces from the late Sir Henry Hartley. You are also charged under Sections 16, 17, and 33 of the Births and Deaths Registration Act of 1953 that you failed to inform the Registrar of Births and Deaths of Hartley's death. Do you plead Guilty or Not Guilty?'

'Not Guilty.'

The police prosecutor, an inspector in uniform, rose and said, 'Your worships, I ask for a remand for one week by which time the police expect to be in a position to state when the case can proceed. Some of the papers are being sent to the Director of Public Prosecutions this afternoon.'

'The case is remanded for one week,' the white-haired chairman of the magistrates announced. 'Do you ask for bail?' he said to Williams.

'Yes please, I do. Indeed I would like that.'

'Any objection?' the chairman asked the prosecutor.

'None, your worship.'

The chairman's two colleagues nodded their assent, and he said to Williams, 'You're granted bail on your own surety of £100. Do you accept that?'

'Thank you, I do.'

The usher beckoned Williams from the dock and told him in a whisper where to go, and Bird, listening from a side bench, followed him out of court to show him the ropes about signing the surety form and so on. The court-room door had hardly closed behind them when it burst open again and out came the sole reporter present. He looked at Bird who shook his head, and he looked at Williams and began hopefully, 'Captain, will you tell me – '

'He's saying nothing,' Bird answered for him. 'There's no police statement either.'

Defeated for the moment but undismayed the reporter left them, ran out of the police station, and sprinted to the nearest public telephone. He was wanting to tell his news editor he was on to a real scoop.

After sending Williams home in a police car Bird rang up the Coroner to say that so far as the police were concerned Hartley's inquest could now proceed to its conclusion, no evidence having been found to establish death was due to anything other than natural causes. At the same time Bird thanked him for all his help and promised once he got back to headquarters to clear the files by confirming in writing.

And that's that, Bird said to himself, and applied his mind to other matters. Of these the most pressing were where to stop and shop in Bromborough and whether to buy sausage or fish fillets for tonight's supper. He also found himself envying Williams for having a woman to cook for him.

2

(November 14 & later)

That same morning the Stipendiary of Liverpool meted out much the same treatment to Gosling, the difference in his case being that bail was fixed on a personal surety of £500 together with a second surety for the same amount, and subject to his passport being handed over to the police.

Hence Gosling was not released until the late afternoon because the first pilot friend approached expressed unwillingness to stand and the second proved to be unavailable – as a matter of fact he was playing poker in

the saloon of No 2 Pilot Boat off Point Lynas while awaiting his turn on the inward rota. In the end it was Captain
Armstrong who, having heard of the dilemma, volunteered to come to Y Division and give surety. And, since
neither Gosling nor the Liverpool police were saying
anything, the press was again thwarted. Muzzled too,
because Detective Inspector Richardson was not slow
in reminding the several reporters who excitedly
gathered round him as he left the Stipendary's court
that they'd better watch their step as the case was
sub judice.

Thus the best that evening's *Echo* could achieve was
the banner headline SAMARAI SENSATION – CAP-
TAIN AND PILOT CHARGED and beneath it the
bare news that Walter Gosling, a Mersey pilot, had been
charged at Dale Street with conspiring with the late Sir
Henry Hartley to defraud the Trident Marine and other
insurance companies of £795,000, that Walter Gosling
had been further charged with conspiring with Captain
Ifor Williams of Rock Ferry to demand money with
menaces from Sir Henry Hartley, and that Walter Gosling and Captain Williams had also been charged with
concealing Sir Henry Hartley's death. Both men, the
paragraph concluded in the nature of an anticlimax, had
been remanded for one week on bail.

This was big stuff even by the standards of the blasé
modern world, and on Wednesday morning every national newspaper in the land, several continental ones
too, picked up the *Samarai* story from its simple start and
left millions of their readers tantalized and guessing.
Only word of mouth on Liverpool dockland dared to
reveal the real truth – that those three fellahs, having
sunk their bloody ship, had had a proper blarney, and
the only reason one of them wasn't inside for bashing
Hartley up was because each was trying to shop the other

and the scuffers couldn't yet make up their minds which had done him.

Committal proceedings began at once in their respective courts when Gosling and Williams reappeared a week later, and at the end of a long and wearisome day – the law at that time decreed that every word of committal proceedings must be recorded as it was being spoken – the two men were sent for trial, bail again being granted on the same terms as before. Each man, now in the guiding hands of his chosen solicitor, had pleaded Not Guilty and reserved his defence.

At this stage the Director of Public Prosecutions stepped in. All indictable offences of the kind which Gosling and Williams were accused had to be referred to him, and Bird – concerned only with the case against Williams – twice visited his office in Buckingham Gate to consult one of his assistants. For the Chief Constable of Cheshire held the view that Williams, however reprehensible his conduct and misconceived it had been, was speaking the truth when in his statement he declared his attempt to blackmail Hartley had been motivated solely by his desire to establish Hartley's guilt, and in consequence the Chief Constable was ready to drop the more serious charge against him and proceed only with the minor one of failing to notify Hartley's death. However the Director ruled that on grounds of public policy Williams must stand trial on both charges, the question of his guilt or otherwise being left to a jury to decide.

The Director also ruled that both men were to be tried, though not necessarily side by side, at the same assize in Liverpool, a sensible decision which as well as easing the machinery of administration would save the police a good deal of time and the ratepayers of Cheshire several thousand pounds. Apart from one or two barristers on the Chester and North Wales Circuit no one objected – least of all Williams, who seemed curiously blind to his position and was devoting more and more time to his stamps.

Soon after the end of the committal proceedings Richardson took a significant step. Having got his man he was now anxious to do what he could to help him, and accompanied by Mrs Richardson he paid an evening visit to the Gosling household. He also wished to help Williams, and with this in mind contrived to have a private conversation with Mrs Gosling, considering her to be the dominant partner. To save the susceptibilities of those who hold that justice is sacrosanct and must not suffer interference, it is as well that what he suggested to her, and what she undertook to do for him, has never leaked. The visit was successful in other ways too; Gosling, though reserved, showed no hostility to Richardson and the two wives struck up a friendship which endures to this day.

The weeks dragged on and Christmas came and went. Defence counsel were briefed. *Regina v. Gosling* and *Regina v. Williams* were set down for hearing at the forthcoming assizes. Press and Bar alike were now poised for what in the annals of Liverpool crime seemed likely to be a *cause célèbre*. The prosecution raised a minor ripple in the legal pond by advising the defence that the charge of demanding money with menaces would be withdrawn if Gosling pleaded Guilty to the other two charges.

When told of this Gosling shrugged his shoulders and said nothing except to his solicitor; like many another man or woman awaiting trial he only wanted to get it over. His solicitor kept his mouth shut too; thus no outsider knew if the conversations about to take place in chambers between solicitor and counsel would be restricted to what could be said in mitigation of sentence.

In Williams's case the situation was different. His counsel, an ebullient man, had gone deeply into the whole extraordinary affair and announced to one or two Bar colleagues that given the right judge and an intelligent jury he expected to get his man off. But he modified his opinion on hearing that owing to the sudden illness of Mr Justice Cunsey the trial judge was likely to be Mr Justice Twist. For Mr Justice Twist, though an able and senior judge, was known to dislike criminal cases; he travelled on circuit with his violincello and without his wife, and his quirks were so legendary that few young barristers would have elected to be his marshal.

3

In No 1 Court of St George's Hall at the January assizes Walter Gosling, having been arraigned on two charges and having pleaded Guilty to both, stood in the dock while his counsel addressed Mr Justice Twist for eight and a quarter minutes.

The judge then fixed his cold eyes on the prisoner and said, 'I have listened with care to what has been said on your behalf, but I cannot think any the better of you or of the wicked plot to which you have been a party. I accept that you were induced to play your part in this conspiracy by a personality more powerful and perhaps more evil than yourself, but the fact remains that without your skilled and willing help the conspiracy must have failed. Your counsel has pleaded that the conspiracy did fail, in so far as the insurance companies, suspecting fraudulent intent, withheld payment of claims. To this I must add it was due only to the zeal and ability of the two police officers concerned that these insurance companies have now been finally absolved. Nor can I forget that the public body responsible for the safety of shipping in the waters over which it has jurisdiction is compelled to meet a heavy bill of costs for removing the obstruction which your action has brought about.

'Your counsel has also pleaded that you have received no monetary reward for the dubious service you rendered to your employer. That may well be so, but I have yet to learn by what process of reasoning the loss of ill-gotten gains may be construed to mean the deprived recipient is thereby deserving of sympathy. However I do take note of your counsel's observation that by your momentary lapse, as he saw fit to describe it, you have wrecked for all time your hitherto exemplary career. For my part I remind you that you should have borne this in mind before you wrecked the ship entrusted to your care.

'It is to your credit that you confessed your crime and have pleaded Guilty to the two charges against you. One is relatively trivial and its circumstances are such that I direct it be left on the file. For your other offence, which undermines the very roots of the maritime and commercial integrity which it is my duty to uphold, you must go to prison for five years.'

4

No 1 Court was equally crowded two days later when *Regina v. Williams* was heard before Mr Justice Twist. Defendant's counsel was Evan Evans Q.C.

Though opening with his usual excessive confidence, Bottomley Q.C., counsel for the Crown, did not feel happy about his brief. For one thing the accused, a respectable citizen by his record, seemed guilty of nothing worse than of having behaved like an incredible ass;

for another the Crown's only witness – unless Evan was intending to subject his client to the risks of cross-examination by putting him in the box – was a convicted criminal, and trust Evan to lose not a moment in tearing apart his character, his veracity too. A most curious case in every way. Bottomley was reflecting, as fluently and lucidly and on this occasion speaking in an almost conversational voice, he outlined to the jury the story which he promised would shortly be proved to the hilt.

In the eyes of criminal law, he told them, the fact that the prisoner in the dock would no doubt be claiming that his motives were pure made not one iota of difference. Demanding money with menaces was an atrocious crime, and the jury must dismiss from their minds anything they had heard or read which induced them to believe that the man whom the prisoner was accused of having blackmailed had rendered himself – to use modern parlance – 'fair game' by allegedly being guilty of a crime himself. Dead men could tell no tales, in other words Hartley was no longer able to defend himself. This was a simple story of greed or malice, perhaps both, being applied to right an imagined wrong, and the jury would soon hear how the prisoner had compiled an astonishing document in which he revealed step by step the method he had devised to bring his foul purpose to fruition. The jury would also hear how the prisoner, when the meeting which he had engineered actually took place, demanded the by no means derisory sum of one thousand pounds as the value he placed upon his silence. Such were the facts, the indisputable facts, so he believed, and if the jurors were ready to judge a man not by his explanations or excuses but by his actions he could confidently leave it to them to form their own conclusions regarding the prisoner's guilt.

Conscious that perhaps half the jurors were impressed,

Bottomley Q.C. brought out one of his more telling mannerisms by mopping his forehead with his red silk handkerchief just before he sat down. While pocketing it he gazed for a split second at the judge sitting impassive on his throne and wondered if he too thought the case against Williams pretty thin.

'Call Walter Gosling,' the clerk of the court ordered, and the court usher, an ex-sergeant-major, obeyed in a parade-ground voice loud enough to make the judge wince.

Brought up from below, Gosling took his stand in the witness box – he had been kept handy in Walton Prison since having been sentenced two days earlier. Though his hair had been cut short he was not dressed in prison uniform, and several in the press box jotted down he looked sallow and seemed self-possessed.

The clerk of the court intoned like a well-worn gramophone record, 'Take the oath please and say after me, "I swear by Almighty God that the evidence I shall give ... shall be the truth ... the whole truth and nothing but the truth ..."'

'You are Walter Gosling?' Mr Bottomley Q.C. began, on his feet again.

'I am.'

'Were you present in Williams's house in Rock Ferry on Tuesday October 25 when Sir Henry Hartley arrived there at about a quarter past six?'

'I was.'

'Am I correct in saying you had arranged this meeting yourself?'

'Yes.'

'Why had you arranged it?'

'Because Williams asked me to.'

'In consequence of something he had said to you about a week previously?'

'Yes.'

'Did he then say' – Bottomley was reading from a photostat of Williams's précis attached to his proof of evidence – ' "Do we not owe it to ourselves to put our heads together and persuade Sir Henry Hartley to treat each of us more generously?" '

This was so nearly a leading question that Bottomley was half expecting it to be disallowed. But the judge let it pass and Evan Evans did not protest because at that moment the defence solicitor behind him was leaning forward to whisper in his ear he had just learned from an impeccable source that something highly dramatic was in the wind.

'Yes, he did say that. Or something very like it.'

'And how did this meeting you had arranged begin?'

'By Williams kind of welcoming Sir Henry.'

Someone in court tittered, and Bottomley showed he did not like it. 'Towards the end of this address of welcome what exactly did Williams say to Sir Henry?'

'I can't remember.'

'You can't remember?' Bottomley was glancing at his instructions which under the head of GOSLING WILL SAY contained the words, 'He demanded one thousand pounds from him.' 'Come now, let me ask you again.'

'It's no good asking me again. I mean I'm not going to remember.'

Bottomley turned towards the judge and raised his eyes in eloquent appeal.

'The question you have been asked is a perfectly proper one and you must answer it,' Mr Justice Twist told Gosling sternly.

'I'm sorry, my Lord, but I'm saying nothing against Williams.'

The judge became severe. 'Let me get this clear. Is the position that you refuse to testify?'

184

'Yes, my Lord. I've been thinking a lot about all this and – '

'What you think is of no interest whatsoever. By refusing to testify you are committing a contempt of court for which – ' the judge stopped short as he saw no point in adding 'I can send you to prison' to a man to whom he had just given five years.

'I'm not meaning anything like that, my Lord. It's only that I think Williams is a wronged and honest man – '

'Be silent!' the judge ordered, and turned to Mr Bottomley. 'Do you wish to question this witness further?'

'I am embarrassed and have to ask for your Lordship's indulgence to enable me to take instructions.'

The judge nodded wearily and closed his eyes. Hoping in vain to quell the hum of excitement rising from press box and public gallery alike, the usher opened his mouth and bellowed, 'SILENCE IN COURT!'

Meantime Mr Bottomley, contorting his big body and bewigged head to confront the prosecuting solicitor seated immediately behind him, was saying, 'Why the devil couldn't you have found this out yesterday when you saw him in Walton?' To which the solicitor answered, 'I'm every bit as shaken as you are. I'm sure his wife's responsible for this, she was waiting to go in when I came out and looked straight through me. And I saw her here this morning talking to the defence.' 'Whatever the reason you've made a bloody fool of me,' Mr Bottomley retorted. 'What's more I won't – '

Known throughout the legal world as an impatient man, the judge was inquiring, 'Now, Mr Bottomley, how nearly are you ready?'

'I am now, my Lord ... Er, I see no point in continuing to press this witness.'

'Then let him stand down and call your next.'

'There are no more, my Lord.'

'This being the whole of the Crown case?'

'Not entirely ... Though it would appear to have become so, and in the circumstances I am unable to carry it further.'

Evan Evans Q.C. rose, but without undue haste. 'My Lord, I submit the defendant has no case to answer.'

'I agree with you. Perhaps Mr Bottomley agrees too?'

Mr Bottomley nodded with histrionic indignation.

Addressing the jury, the judge said, 'I direct you to find the prisoner Not Guilty.' Looking down at the clerk of the court, he told him, 'The second charge will remain on the file.'

The judge's marshal, a slim and decorative young man, slipped out of court through the judge's door to prepare the whisky and soda he knew his Lordship would shortly be requiring. The foreman of the jury, bewildered by the turn of events, needed prompting by the usher before he could announce, 'Not Guilty, my Lord.'

'You are discharged and may go,' Mr Justice Twist told Williams.

As bewildered as the foreman of the jury, Williams said, 'I do not quite understand.'

The court was overheated and very noisy. The judge, as resentful of the wasted hour as he was conscious of the length of the calendar before him and aware of his immediate need for a drink, said testily, 'Don't you understand English? The jury has found you Not Guilty.'

'Not Guilty? That is what I have been saying too! ... Indeed I have always been on the side of the police!' In his elation Williams burst into Welsh, 'Mae hyn yn

186

dangos bod cyfiawnder i Gymro yn Lloegr!'

As Captain Williams stepped out of the dock Evan Evans Q.C. gave him the V sign. Bottomley Q.C., gathering together his papers, nudged Evans in the stomach and muttered in ill temper, 'You speak his language presumably. What did he say?'

Evan Evans placed his arm round the shoulders of his disgruntled friend – after all were they not Benchers of the same Inn? – and replied, 'Don't worry, old man. He only said, "This shows a Welshman can have justice in England."'

This ends the narrative, but the reader is invited to turn to the four pages which follow.

Copy of letter from the Director of Public Prosecutions to the Chief Constable of Liverpool:

'Samarai'

Thank you for your letter of yesterday's date enclosing particulars about the results of this interesting and unusual case.

The only comment I have to make is to compliment you and the C.I.D. officers concerned on the immense amount of time spent and trouble taken to solve this mystery.

I am, Sir,
Your obedient Servant,
M—— R——

Liverpool has not been standing still during the fifteen years which now have passed since Gosling grounded the Samarai *on the Mersey Revetment, and though at the moment its image as a great seaport has become slightly tarnished let no one imagine its inherited skills and magnetism will not prevail. In the meantime a million Liverpudlians have ample compensation – is not their city renowned and esteemed throughout the world for its two Division 1 football clubs and as having been the nursery and home-town of the Beatles?*

The New Guinea Steamship Company went into compulsory liquidation twelve years ago and has vanished from the Merseyside scene. Two of its ships are still afloat, but bear different names. Its offices in India Buildings did not remain empty long; they are still as busy as they used to be. They were taken on long lease by the Inland Revenue. The Company's pension fund is still of course intact; its surviving beneficiaries include Captain Beecher and Miss Webb.

By marrying again within six months of her husband's death Sir Henry's widow lost her title and became Mrs Piper-Penthouse, her second husband being the well-known army and gentleman rider of that name. On his retirement from the Royal Artillery the Brigadier and his wife went to live in Malta, and inside the Christmas card I received from her a year or two ago she had written, perhaps not very grammatically, 'This is the only remaining corner of our one-time Empire still fit for the poor to end their days in.'

Like his old friend Captain Armstrong, Captain Williams died a few years ago. Both continued as members of the *Landfall*, and they lunched there together from time to time. According to Captain Armstrong, Captain Williams never mentioned the *Samarai*.

Mrs Williams sold the stamps and the Rock Ferry house – but not the OBE – which the Captain had left to her, and did quite well out of them. She is now the housekeeper of Detective Chief Inspector Bird; they had first met when Bird – a widower it will be remembered – called at the house to question her. But may I make it clear she is Bird's housekeeper and nothing else, and is still known as Mrs Williams.

The Goslings live in Jersey where they more than make ends meet by selling the tomatoes which they grow professionally under glass. Their daughter Margaret became engaged the other day – by a curious coincidence to one of the Thames pilots. As often as not the Richardsons fly to Jersey for their spring holiday and still keep in touch with them all.

Chief Inspector Young grows tomatoes too, but only from a couple of dozen plants and just as a hobby. He has a small cold greenhouse in his garden in Bridge of Allen. He was born up there, and though a Liverpool girl his wife stood by her promise to live in Scotland after he retired. I understand she now quite likes it.

Bob Richardson left the Liverpool police seven years ago, when, having previously been promoted to Chief Inspector, he was appointed Chief Constable of one of the several Merseyside Boroughs. Due to the recent and drastic reduction in the number of smaller police forces he has had to revert to the rank of Assistant Chief Constable. But why worry, he says, the main thing's being happy in your work. His son Copper, who joined the Metropolitan Police, is now attending the 12-month course for up-and-coming young sergeants at the National Police College at Bramshill in Hampshire.

Arthur Bernard, the plump shipbroker and ex-member of the Dockboard who by his chance remark to Malcolm McGregor – now Sir Malcolm McGregor – still claims to have triggered off the police inquiry, is on friendly terms with Richardson. Now retired himself, he said to Richardson a year or two ago, 'You've already written a book about one of your cases, that one about the Drummer and the Doctor and the gang of toughs who'd all been street musicians. So why not write another about the *Samarai*?'

Richardson laughed and shook his head. 'I'm writing no more books while still in the police,' he replied. 'I got a lot of stick from my Chief Constable over the one you mention. The Watch Committee didn't like it either ... But hold on a moment – why not *you*? You're out of the rat-race now and always complaining you haven't

enough to do. So what about me giving you all the facts and you writing it for me?'

And that, believe it or not, is how the story of the *Samarai* came to have been written.